A LEGACY OF HOPE

DARREN CHITWOOD

A Legacy of Hope
Copyright ©2020 by Darren Chitwood
All rights reserved.

Sifton, Elisabeth. **The Serenity Prayer**: Faith and Politics in Times of Peace and War. New York: Norton, 2003. Print.

All Scripture quotations, unless otherwise indicated, are taken from the Holy Bible, New International Version®, NIV®. Copyright ©1973, 1978, 1984, 2011 by Biblica, Inc.™ Used by permission of Zondervan. All rights reserved worldwide. www.zondervan.com. The "NIV" and "New International Version" are trademarks registered in the United States Patent and Trademark Office by Biblica, Inc.™

ISBN (Print): 978-0-578-76592-1

ISBN (eBook): 978-0-578-76593-8

Cover design: Luísa Dias, *LuisaDias.com*

Editing: Lisa Vest

Formatting: Lois McKiernan, *StudioMercy.com*

❀ Created with Vellum

CHAPTER ONE

A s Sarah walked through the fruity scent of e-cigarette vapor, the light beat of the music reverberated through her chest, coursing through her veins, causing her to dance to its rhythm as she waited for the bartender's attention. It was a late, Friday afternoon at Mic's Pub in Chicago, and Sarah ordered another round of beer for her friends.

Friday nights were her typical time to unwind and to spend time with friends. She found the slight buzz from the alcohol and the accompanying laughter and dance a wonderful way to spend her evenings. And even though she uncharacteristically agreed to take on a shift at the hospital the following morning, she was unwilling to put off this weekly ritual.

She had frequented Mic's Pub for the last three years and had become well acquainted with its owners and knew all the bartenders by name. With all the openness that inebriation brings, she joked they should send her bills for her counseling sessions.

As she continued to dance to the 70's rock music, she

noticed one of the bartenders finishing up an order for a patron. "Hey, Rodney. C'mon. I don't have all night. I gotta group of friends who are dyin' for another round of beer. Can you help a lady out?"

Rodney rolled his eyes, used to the friendly banter with Sarah. "Hey, don't think I haven't forgotten about Ron's tab. He still owes me some money from last week."

"Oh, c'mon Rodney. You know he's good for it. Here," she said, reaching into her purse. "I can tell this has been an emotional evening for you, as usual. I've been telling you that you should find a new line of work. I know how stressful the demands of this job have been on you," she said, wiping away pretend tears. "Now please, don't go cryin' on me again. I tell you what. How 'bout I pay off his tab and pay for another round of beers. Hell, looks like you could use one as well. Why don't you take a break and join us?" she said, unable to keep a grin from her face.

"You know," Rodney said, "now that I think about it, why don't you throw in another 20 for all the grief you have given me this last hour. As you can see, I'm still this handsome, young, studly man, and your constant badgering is already creating lines on this beautiful piece of work," he said, pointing to his face.

As Rodney continued to talk, she noticed her phone vibrate. Attempting to answer it, she noticed a man approach from her peripheral vision.

"Hey, how are you?" asked the older man, with grayish, slick-backed hair. "You look like you could use some company. How about a drink?"

Sarah gently shook her head, quickly exchanging a grin with Rodney.

Smiling at the man, she said, "Well, honey, if you were so

perceptive, you would've known that I've been sitting over there," she said pointing at the booth where her friends sat talking. "And you would've noticed that large man sitting at the end of the booth. His name's Ron, and he's my boyfriend. I'm sure the two of you would like to meet."

"Oh no... sorry," said the man. "I didn't know..."

"It's okay. It's no problem. Like you said, you didn't know. But why don't you take your perceptive nature and direct it towards someone else. Okay?"

She shook her head and watched as the man walked away, unable to suppress a laugh.

Having spent most of her adult life in the bar scene, Sarah had her fair share of advances from men. The worst one happened when a married man tried to slip his phone number to her while his wife used the restroom. She simply turned her back to him and walked away. Creep, she thought. It was one of the realities of the bar-life, she thought.

She felt her phone vibrate again. Reaching down, she noticed it was an email from her aunt, Mindy. What in the world could she want? she whispered to herself.

There had been an argument several years ago regarding Sarah's son, and Mindy had sent a harsh and judgmental letter to Sarah. It escalated to the point that Sarah stopped all contact with her, even blocking her phone number. Curious, she opened the email.

Sarah, I've tried contacting you several times by phone and haven't received a response, so I'm emailing you. Honey, your Dad has passed away! Please call me. I'm so sorry to have to tell you this. I know we haven't had the greatest relationship, but I don't want to have to tell you everything in writing. We should talk over the phone. Please call! I'm worried. You won't return my calls. Please, at least acknowledge that you received this email. I'll be waiting to hear from you. Love, Mindy.

"Hey, is everything all right?" Rodney called out as he got her order ready.

"Oh, yeah, everything's okay," Sarah said, struggling to regain her composure. "I just need to go to the bathroom."

As Sarah sat alone in the restroom in front of the sink, she read over the email again, trying to process what she had read. She hadn't spoken to her dad in years, and the news took her completely by surprise.

She looked in the mirror at her long, auburn hair that fell gently over her eyebrows and flowed mid-way down her back. Her large, hazel eyes stared back at her behind her tortoise colored glasses and began to brim with tears. Embarrassed, she quickly removed her glasses and washed her face.

Just then, her friend, Patricia walked into the bathroom. "Hey Sarah, what's wrong? Are you okay?" she said as she reached out her hand to touch Sarah's shoulder.

Sarah instinctively drew back, collecting her thoughts before saying, "I'm fine, Patricia. I don't really want to talk about it, but something's come up. I need to get home."

"Wait, Sarah, what's going on? This is not like you. You know you can talk to me, right?" she said as she looked Sarah straight in her eyes.

"Patricia, really, it's okay. I just found out something…" She stopped herself, turning her gaze as she faced her palms out towards her friend. Clearing her throat, she said, "Please, can you tell everyone that something's come up and I had to leave? Just trust me. I'm okay."

"Sarah, don't you think…?"

"Patricia, can you please do that for me? I really need to get

4

home. And tell Ron not to worry, okay? I'll send him a text later tonight."

Sarah quickly waved down a taxi in the brisk, Chicago air. With her nursing salary, she lived comfortably in a condominium in the heart of the city where she could be in the midst of the action and be close to her work, so it only took a few minutes to arrive home.

As she walked upstairs to her room, her eyes paused on a picture frame that displayed a series of photos of her son from 1st through 12th grade. The last picture was the largest of all, showing a handsome, smiling young man, who proudly displayed a recently grown mustache.

With everything that had happened in the last hour, she couldn't stop thinking about her son, David, and she wanted nothing more than to hold him in her arms. Silly, she thought. He's a grown man. Besides, it was late, and he was probably asleep. She quickly changed her clothes and walked downstairs.

Alone in her kitchen, Sarah sat staring at the crystal vase she was given at a Christmas party years before. As she stared through the glass, which cast prisms of light throughout the room, she felt overcome with feelings of sadness and hopelessness. She felt trapped, like a caged lion, fighting for its life, but she didn't know who to attack, so she turned her feelings inward. Taking a deep breath and slowly letting it out, she continued to stare at the vase, hoping this would somehow ease her mind.

Sarah thought she had dealt with these emotions long ago when she sought help with therapists in her early 20s. It all started with a reoccurring dream where she was a girl hearing her parents fight in their bedroom. She didn't know what they were arguing about, but her mom continually screamed, "Help me, Sarah. Please help me!" As Sarah approached the bedroom, the hallway would stretch and contort, so that no matter how fast she ran, she could never reach her mom, but she could always hear her mother's voice as if she were next to her.

The first few sessions were easy because she only had to talk about her life and career, keeping things on a superficial level. But as the counseling progressed, the therapist would attempt to dig deeper into her childhood to examine the root causes of her issues. "How did your father and mother treat you?" they would ask. "Did you have a good relationship with them?" She never knew why, but she couldn't answer these questions and became defensive. It was simply too painful, so after a few sessions, she would move on to the next counselor.

She remembered one meeting when the therapist gently told her that she had anxiety and abandonment issues. Sarah was so angry that she stated the woman had no idea what she was talking about and stood up in the middle of the session and left the woman's office. She resolved never to see a therapist again and believed that nobody could help her. She had even tried medication, but with its horrible side-effects of nausea and dizziness, she stopped that as well. Nothing and no one could help, she kept telling herself, and she believed all she had was herself.

Hadn't she been top of her class in nursing school with a toddler at home? She hadn't even had family to take care of her son as some of her classmates had with their children. Convinced that she was strong enough to handle any uncomfortable emotions that surfaced, she isolated herself from anyone who could possibly help.

This approach seemed to have worked. It had been years since she had sought help, and the anxiety and sadness were kept at bay - until this evening. Now everything had suddenly changed. The unexpected email from her aunt affected her in ways she wasn't ready to deal with.

She read the email over and over again to make sure she understood it correctly. What was she going to do? After what seemed like an eternity, she summoned the courage to google her father's name and found an obituary from a small town she had never heard of in Northern California:

Thomas Lynn Martin, age 67, died on November 28th, 2019 from complications of Pancreatic Cancer. He is survived by his daughter, Sarah Martin. His loss is felt deeply by our small rural community, who loved him very much. As Deacon and member of the Church Board for First Baptist Church, he was best known for his outreach services. He created connections with the neediest in our society by providing food and clothing to our homeless.

Thomas's greatest strength was to motivate others to serve. He wanted our church congregation to live out their faith – not just to profess it in church Sunday mornings. He always led by example. He was the most generous man our community has known, and count-less lives have been touched because of him.

Memorial services will be held this Saturday, December 7th at First Baptist Church at 2:00 pm. All of those whose lives were touched by this man are invited to come. In lieu of sending flowers, we ask that you send food and clothing donations to our church so that we may keep Thomas' name alive through our giving.

It was 2:00 in the morning, and she would need to get up for work in just a few hours. Considering whether she should call in sick, Sarah looked outside and noticed small flakes of snow, lit by the streetlights as they fell gently to the ground. According to the forecast, there would be upwards of six to eight inches by dawn. As she looked at her empty bed, she real-ized Ron still had not arrived home, and she hadn't received a text from him.

She went to the bathroom and stared at herself long in the mirror. "It's not important," she kept repeating to herself. "Life must go on. It's just the way it is. Everyone dies." And after some time in silence, she collected herself and took a long, hot shower, but not before deleting and blocking her aunt's email.

CHAPTER TWO

The week at *Family Camp* was coming to an end as the youth sat around the campfire late Thursday evening. It was the second to last day of camp, and the air was permeated with the sounds of guitars and singing and the occasional popping of embers from the fire. The slight breeze occasionally shifted, directing smoke to different parts of the audience who slightly coughed as they continued to sing. Looking up, the clear starry sky was obscured by the enormous Redwood trees, whose branches intertwined with one another, as if locked in an eternal embrace.

Sarah was twelve and sat down next to her best friend Rebecca. They held hands as one of the leaders shared his testimony, discussing his involvement in gangs and drugs, and how God had miraculously changed his life. One could hear sniffles amongst the audience as the speaker gave an altar call. Sarah stood up, urging her friend to follow her. The two girls got up and walked down by the fire, still holding hands, publicly making a commitment to their new way of life.

"Look, he's got decreased breath sounds on his right side. He may have a collapsed lung. We need an X-Ray up here, and get me a chest tube tray immediately," Dr. Danheiser barked out at the nurses in the ICU as he looked at the eight-year-old boy.

"Sarah," he said, shaking his head. "I'm disappointed in you. I should've known about this earlier. His heart rate is 130. What were you thinking?"

"I'm sorry Dr. Danheiser. I just wanted to give it a few more minutes…"

"Not now. I don't have time. We need to prep the child."

One of the nurses scrambled to get the chest tube, sterile gloves, and gown for the doctor, while Sarah pulled down the patient's gown, prepping his skin with betadine.

"Give me the patient's vital signs," Dr. Danheiser said as he inserted the chest tube.

"Pulse ox level is at 85%. Heart rate is now at 150. His blood pressure is 80/60," Sarah said, glancing down at the boy. He was so young, with thick, wavy, blond-hair, plastered against his forehead, and dimples on his cheeks. She couldn't help but think of her son.

"I almost got the chest tube in," the doctor said. "Give him some more fluids."

The ventilator continued to make a whistling noise, detecting abnormal pressure in the patient's airway as the respiratory tech managed its settings. "I need those fluids," the doctor again called out.

"How much?" Sarah said.

"400 ccs of normal saline should suffice."

"Come on, young man," Dr. Danheiser said, as he finished inserting the chest tube. "You're going to make it. I know you are. Your family needs you."

The child looked so innocent as he lay unconscious on the hospital bed, out of place in the sterile room, brightly lit by fluorescent lights. The vinyl floor carried the echoes of the IV's giving medication to patients and the beeping heart monitors registering patient's vitals throughout the floor.

"I need his vitals, Sarah" Dr. Danheiser called out.

"Pulse ox level is 87%, and the heart rate is 140. Blood pressure is 90/70."

"Come on, Daniel," the doctor said again, laying his hand gently on the boy's chest. "You've got your whole life ahead of you, and your mother needs you. You're gonna make it. I know you're gonna make it…"

———————

"WHAT AN INTENSE MORNING THIS HAS BEEN," GRACE SAID AS she sat across Sarah at a table in the cafeteria. "That poor little boy," she said as she ate her salad.

As she sipped her hot cocoa, Sarah stared at the line of people at the buffet table. Looking over at Grace, she said, "Yeah, the mother's hand wouldn't stop shaking when Dr. Danheiser came out to the waiting room to talk to her. I thought she was going to faint. Then she went over to her son and buried her face in his lap and started praying for him. It was just too much… I had to leave."

"Sarah, I've been doin' this work for at least 10 years longer than you, and I don't care how calloused you think you get. Seeing an innocent, young boy fighting for his life, never gets easy. You never get used to that. My boys a grown man with a family of his own, but all I could think about this morning was my Franky hooked up to that ventilator, fighting for his life."

Grace put down her utensils and lightly touched Sarah's

forearm. "What's wrong, honey? You're crying. What's the matter?"

Knowing how private Sarah was, Grace was tempted to change the topic to a lighter subject, but she felt she needed to press the issue. "Sarah, what's going on?"

Sarah was quiet for a moment, struggling with whether or not to open up to her friend on such a personal issue. "I got an email from my aunt this morning. I hadn't heard from her in a long time, and she told me that my dad died."

"I'm sorry," Grace said, as she placed her hand on top of Sarah's.

"Don't worry about it, Grace," Sarah said, removing her hand. "I didn't know him that well, and I haven't spoken to him in many years."

Grace kept silent a few moments, with her arms open as she looked at Sarah.

"Will there be a memorial service?"

"Yes," Sarah replied. "I read his obituary online, and it said there would be a service on Saturday the seventh."

"Are you planning on going?"

"I'm not sure. I didn't know him very well, and I'm needed here at the hospital."

"Sarah. I understand from the little you've told me that you didn't have the closest relationship with your dad, but if I were you, I would do everything possible to go to that service. Honey, take some time off work – hell, take off a whole week. Life's short. Trust me, you don't want to miss this opportunity to say goodbye. You may regret it for the rest of your life."

Sarah briefly considered what Grace said as she leaned her elbow on the table and rested her chin in her hand.

"You don't know this about me, Sarah but my father was a drug addict. He abandoned the family and deeply hurt me and my siblings in so many ways. For most of my adult life, I didn't want anything to do with him, but a few years ago he reached out to me. He was dying and wanted to make amends."

As Sarah listened to her friend, she looked down at the ground as her right foot made a brushing movement along the floor.

"I wasn't sure what to do," said Grace, "so I opened up to a friend. She encouraged me to talk to my father and even offered to be there in the hospital room for emotional support. She was there, holding my hand as I confronted the man I'd hated for so many years. I don't think I could've done it without her. I'm deeply grateful that I listened to my friend."

"Sarah, I know your father has already passed, and maybe he didn't treat you the way my father did, but I would hate for you to regret not saying your goodbyes at his memorial service."

They sat in silence for a few moments as Sarah processed her friend's story. Minutes later, they got up from the table to return to their shifts as Grace said, "Sarah if you ever need somebody to talk to, you know where I am."

When Sarah arrived home that evening, she found Ron on the couch watching the playoffs. He was lying on the couch in his underwear when he jumped up and gave a fist bump in the air. Turning around, he seemed surprised at Sarah's presence. "Oh, hey honey," he said, quickly turning his attention back to the game.

He rubbed his unshaven face and his clothes smelled like a combination of sweat and fast-food. Sarah knew she would probably be right to assume he had barely moved off the couch all day except to eat and go to the restroom. She stopped asking about his job search because she would always get the same response: *I just haven't found the right fit for me.*

She went to the kitchen to decide what to prepare for dinner. "Hey Ron, I need to talk to you about something."

Ron leaped up from the couch. "You're full of shit, ref. Go to hell!"

"Ron," Sarah shouted. "I need to talk to you!"

"Can it wait until half-time?" he asked, not waiting for a response, but going back to his game.

Sarah followed Ron into the living room. "Sorry to interrupt your precious game, but I need to tell you something."

"What?" he asked, visibly annoyed.

"Is that all you have to say? 'Oh, Sarah, what happened to you last night? Where were you? I've been worried sick about you?'"

"Look, Sarah, I don't want to get into this," he said as he glanced at the TV. "Patricia said not to worry and that you would text me or something?"

"Great. I feel so touched by your concern. You know, you could've reached out to me. And where were you last night? You never came home?"

Ron muted the TV. "I…just spent the night at some friend's house. Why don't you tell me what happened last night?"

"Yeah, whatever, Ron. Look,…I found out last night that my dad died, okay? That's why I left the bar early."

She paused, waiting for a response, but continued to speak when she didn't hear anything. "I think I'll be gone for a week. I'm going to his memorial service."

"I guess you gotta do what you gotta do," he said.

Sarah just stared at him.

He dropped his gaze. "I'm sorry to hear about your loss."

The two sat staring at each other in silence for a moment until Sarah left the room. She wouldn't want him to miss his precious game.

After preparing dinner, she went to her room. She needed some space. As she thought about the brief email her aunt had sent her, she kept thinking about what Grace had told her earlier that day: *Trust me, you do not want to miss this opportunity to say goodbye!* She didn't know how to handle the strange emotions that were surfacing, so she quickly turned on the TV to clear her thoughts but after a few minutes turned it off.

She continued in this state of indecisiveness over the next few hours. Annoyed by the incessant thought that she would regret not attending her father's memorial service, she finally said "fine," in desperation to herself.

Downstairs, she heard Ron warming up food in the microwave. As she continued to pace the room, she said aloud, "I'll get the damn round-trip ticket. I'll see where he spent the remaining years of his life. I'll say my damn goodbye. Are you happy?" she asked an unseen adversary.

It was getting late, and she thought about leaving a message with her HR department, but she instead decided to call her supervisor.

"Hey, Sarah," Connie said as she answered her phone. "It's kind of late. Is everything alright?"

"Oh, everything's fine. I'm…I've never asked anything like this before. But I just got news that my father died and was wondering if I could leave as early as tomorrow for his memorial service?"

"I'm sorry to hear that, Sarah. This is so last minute. You okay?"

"I'm fine. I'm sorry for doing this at the last minute… I just found out last night… The service is a few days out, but I feel I need to get there right away."

Connie briefly thought about what Sarah had said. "I know how you feel, Sarah. My mom died suddenly and that was pretty hard on me. I needed to be there with my family right away."

Then after thinking a moment, she said, "I think I can make it work. You've covered for so many people, and I can't think of the last time you missed a shift. Of course, you can go." Then after considering the situation, she said, "Do you need someone to talk to? I'm here if you need me."

Out of everyone at work, Sarah was closest to Connie, but she had opened up very little to her supervisor about her personal life. After considering Connie's question a brief moment, she said, "No, I think I'll be okay. I appreciate your help, though, but I need to start packing."

"Alright," Connie said, knowing the conversation had come to an end. "Just let me know if you need anything, okay?"

Sarah went to the computer and was able to book a round-trip ticket from Chicago, IL to Sacramento, CA. She justified her impulsive decision, reasoning she needed a long-deserved vacation, which she hadn't taken in the last two years.

After a few moments, she reached over for her phone and called her son. When she heard his voicemail, she hung up and decided to text him instead. *David, your grandfather, Thomas, passed away. I just found out this morning. I will be gone for a week. I thought you would want to know. I would love to hear from you, honey.*

She sent the text. As she laid in bed, she routinely swiped at the screen to see if David had replied. There wasn't a response.

CHAPTER THREE

S arah was fifteen. On a rare occasion, her father took her and her best friend Rebecca to the Outback for Sarah's birthday. Rebecca loved Sarah's dad. He had to be one of the funniest people in the world. Sarah went to the restroom. When she came out, she knew something wasn't right. The two were silent and wouldn't make eye contact with her. "Come on, honey, aren't you hungry?" her dad asked. She cautiously went to eat her hamburger, and when she went to take a drink of her soda, nothing came out. "What?" she said. She tried again, even harder, with the same results.

They couldn't handle it any longer as both her dad and Rebecca let out an embarrassingly loud laugh. Their faces turned bright red. With tears coming

down their cheeks, they told her to look inside the straw. Her dad had meticulously stuffed a paper wrapper inside of it while Sarah was in the bathroom. She took out the straw from her cup and blew the wad of paper at his face. Rolling her eyes, she could not help but laugh at her dad.

SARAH ONLY SLEPT FOR ABOUT AN HOUR THAT NIGHT. SHE HAD A strange dream where she showed up to the memorial service and everyone looked at her oddly. "Who are you? Why are you here?" asked a concerned elderly woman Sarah had never met. She felt ashamed and vulnerable. Then the lady suddenly turned on Sarah, shouting: "You don't belong here. Leave."

She awoke, questioning her decision to buy the ticket. She wondered why within the next twenty-four hours she would visit the place her dad had spent the remaining years of his life. "Why am I going?" she kept asking herself but could never come up with a satisfactory answer. She always prided herself at being a careful planner – always thinking things through. Yet here she was, impulsively buying a round trip ticket to a town in which she knew no one. She did not even know where she would stay. "Crazy," she kept repeating to herself. "This is so crazy."

It was 3:30 a.m. as she got out of bed for her 7:00 a.m. flight later that morning. As she sipped her morning coffee, she again looked at her son's pictures in the hallway. She wondered what he would do if she were to pass away. If they lived across the country from one another, would he travel to see her? Would he consider her to have been a good mother? What would he say about her at her memorial service? Who would even show?

She sat in thought for a few moments considering these questions before realizing she needed to get to the train. She looked at the dark, silent house she would leave for the next week as her right hand involuntarily tightened. "It's okay," she told herself. "It will be less than a week. You can do this. You'll be fine."

On her forty-five-minute trip to O'Hare airport on the city's L train, the streets were mostly deserted, except for the snowplows that meticulously cleared the roads for the city's residents who would be using them in just a few hours. In the distance, she saw the top of Willis Tower as she quickly passed by Mic's pub. She imagined Patricia and her other friends having fun while drinking without her throughout the upcoming week, and the idea made her feel lonely.

After checking her luggage and passing through security, she sat silently waiting for her plane's arrival. She looked out at the tarmac in the darkness of the night at an aircraft refueling as a work crew furiously loaded luggage onto a conveyor belt.

Some time had passed, and her plane arrived. She boarded and took her seat, looking out her window to see a crew of men spray the plane's wings to de-ice them. Twenty minutes later, as the airplane lifted into the sky, she saw the bright lights of the city fade as its skyscrapers disappeared, replaced by the immense, profound, and alluring power of Lake Michigan. It was at that moment that the reality of her trip to California hit her. There was no turning back.

Following a short one-hour layover in Colorado, Sarah was able to get some much-needed rest. As the plane began its descent, one of the pilots announced into the intercom. "Over the next thirty minutes, we will be making our descent to Sacramento. Please keep your seatbelts fastened as we are expecting slight turbulence. Thank you again for flying Southwest." Sarah looked out the window and could make out fields below, nicely carved into rectangular sections, like pieces of fabric sewn onto a quilt.

After de-boarding, she got her luggage and went to a rental car agency at the airport to get a vehicle. According to her

GPS, it was approximately two-hundred miles to Burney, a three-hour drive.

As she headed North on I5, she was reminded of a road trip she had taken to Brown County, IN with her father following the death of her grandmother. She vividly remembered that it was fall with oak and maple leaves turning red, brown, and a dull orange as they fell lightly to the ground. They were at Unionville Cemetery, which housed the Little Unionville Church, an old, rural structure built in the late 1800s.

The entire group gathered around the coffin under a large maple tree. Like most of her family, Sarah did not know her grandmother well. Her father rarely spoke about her. But she could tell that he was deeply affected by her death. It was one of the few times in her childhood she remembered seeing him cry. But she knew better than to try to comfort him. He would always push her away.

The first evening was enjoyable. She heard the story of her grandfather cleaning a shotgun in his room when it was accidentally discharged. Fortunately, nobody got hurt except for the family Bible that was underneath the bed. Half of the Old Testament was blown apart. The responses her grandfather gave were that at least the family no longer had to read Leviticus and that now it was indeed the Holy Bible, but Sarah's grandmother didn't find his remarks humorous. It was a valuable keepsake, handed down through multiple generations of men who were preachers, including sermon notes that had meticulously been written in the Bible's margins.

Her grandmother didn't speak to her husband for nearly two weeks, insisting on sleeping in separate rooms. Sarah was surprised by this information. She didn't realize there were preachers in her family line. Her father rarely spoke about religion except to make fun of it. How much more did she not know?

What she remembered most about the trip was the tension amongst the family members, especially between her dad and her aunt Mindy. They had gotten into a heated argument just before the beginning of the service. Sarah did not know the full context of the discussion, but she remembered her aunt saying that she was surprised he had come to the funeral after the way he treated their mother– something about abandonment and him being the cause of their mother leaving their home when he was a teenager.

Sarah was shocked when her dad used some choice words she had never heard him say in public. She had never seen him so angry and instinctively walked in between them to protect her dad. She wanted to express how she felt about what her aunt had said to her father, but she remained quiet. As she reflected on the incident, she still regretted she had not told her aunt Mindy what was truly on her mind.

Sarah slowly gained elevation as she followed Highway 299, a windy mountainous road that led to Burney. There had been an early snowstorm a few days prior causing a light dusting of snow that covered the landscape. To her left, she saw a small section of basalt rock that had been exposed when the land was excavated for the creation of the Highway. To her right, she saw Cedar Creek with its rushing waters that would eventually join the Pit River and in turn the Sacramento.

She was fascinated by a run-down, uninhabitable inn with a tin roof and a double-decker porch that sloped downward from rotting. She imagined what it would have been like in its hay day. As she continued to gain elevation, she noticed huge wind turbines in the distance, slowly rotating by the rush of wind as it blew over the mountain top.

As she descended Hatchet Creek Summit, the fog evaporated, revealing an extensive bare section of ranch land, covered with frost and a lone farmhouse in its center. She drove onto an overlook to take in the scenery. The rolling mountainous terrain was covered with Douglas Fir, Ponderosa, and Sugar Pine trees, which littered the landscape and grew upwards towards the summit of Mt. Burney, an imposing 8,000-foot extinct volcano southeast of the city. Only its summit lay exposed, which was covered in snow.

Further south she could see Freaner and Magee Peak. To her left were electrical lines that cut through the mountain pass and stretched down across the large open field into Burney and continued as far as the eye could see, leaving a section of exposed land in its wake.

After taking in the beauty of the landscape, she continued down the mountain pass. As she entered the city, the highway turned into Main Street, which was the only thoroughfare in the small town of 3,000 residents. The city had one grocery store and a few gas stations. All along the main street were a variety of small businesses, interspersed with resident's homes.

Sarah noticed a deserted church with a For Sale sign off the main road. She was surprised to see a population of homeless and transients, some of whom held out signs either asking for food or a ride. Where did these people stay, she wondered? It was so cold outside.

As she continued to drive, looking for a place to stay, she saw a movie theater, which played only two showings of a single film each day in the afternoons. She drove by the town's bowling alley and saw a family exit their car with their bowling ball bags strapped over their shoulders. It seemed the most popular source of entertainment in town as the entire parking lot was filled with cars.

Most of the restaurants along the main strip looked deserted. She was surprised by how many there were for such a small community. She wondered how the small businesses fared during the offseason when tourism was low and imagined how bustling these places must be during the summer months to remain in business.

As she continued along the road, she came across a few motels. Most looked run-down and deserted. She was wondering if she would ever find a decent place to stay when she approached the Green Meadows Inn. It consisted of several rooms, which were built side by side with green painted gables on each building. Sarah liked the quaint feel of the place. It reminded her of the cabins she stayed in every summer during family camp with her church when she was a girl.

She pulled her car into the parking space in front of the office. She approached the clerk at the desk, a short woman with red hair who looked to be in her 60's. "How may I help you?" asked the lady.

"Yes," said Sarah. "I just got into town and was planning on staying through next Sunday evening."

As the lady entered Sarah's information into the computer, she asked, "What brings you to the area, may I ask? You don't look like the fishing or hunting type."

Sarah faltered for a moment. "I'm here to visit some family," she lied.

"That's wonderful! I know just about everyone in the area, who are they?" Sarah just looked at the woman, not saying anything, and the lady quickly changed to another topic.

"Most people who stop by this time of year are hunters. Elk season just ended, and we are in the middle of deer hunting.

We're also known for our fly fishing," she said as her fingers frantically typed. "Are you much into the outdoors?"

"Not really. I'm just here to see my family," Sarah stated, slightly irritated.

Sensing Sarah's reluctance for small talk, she said, "Your room number is 6. Here's your card. As you go out to your left, it will be the last unit."

"Oh, and by the way, my name's Dorothy. I've lived in this community my entire life and can answer just about any questions you may have about this area. If you need anything, feel free to give a call to the front desk. I hope you have a pleasant stay."

"Thank you," said Sarah, who gathered her luggage and walked to her room.

She was exhausted from all her traveling and quickly fell asleep on her bed. She had a similar dream as the night before in which she was at her father's memorial service. The same elderly woman approached her, asking who she was and why she was there.

"I'm Sarah Martin. Thomas is my father," she said, as she looked down at the lady's feet.

"You liar," the woman shouted. "Who do you think you are interrupting this service?"

All those in attendance stopped what they were doing and in unison shouted to Sarah that she was not welcome – that she had to leave.

"You see, you're not welcome here," the lady sneered. "You never were." As Sarah turned and ran away from the group, she woke up.

It was late morning as she checked her cell phone, disappointed when she had still not received a response from her son, David. She was not at all surprised to have not received even a simple text of "How are you?" or "Did you arrive safely?" from Ron. He probably was too busy watching TV or working out at the gym.

Choosing not to stay cooped up in her motel room, she got in her car to do some more sight-seeing. She looked at the obituary again for the name of the church. It was on the outskirts of town, and as she approached it, she stopped. She did not know why but she couldn't bring herself to drive into the parking lot, let alone go inside. She parked at a distance, looking at the church before turning around and going back to her motel.

In her room, she decided to google the church's number and call. An elderly lady answered. "Thank you for calling First Baptist Church, this is Rose speaking, how may I help you?"

Sarah paused, wondering what she would say.

"Hello, is anyone there?"

"Hi," said Sarah, drawing out the word. "I was calling to confirm the date and time of the memorial service this Saturday."

"Yes, for Thomas Martin. What a wonderful man he was! His death has shaken up our small community. How'd you know him"

"My name's Sarah Martin. He was my father."

Sarah could not believe what she had just said and silently chastised herself. There was a brief silence on the other end of the receiver.

"Oh, bless your heart, young lady. I heard he had a daughter... I'm so glad that you've come. I'm sorry for your loss."

"It's okay," replied Sarah. Her left foot lightly tapped the ground as she took a deep breath. "I guess I just wanted to let people know I was in town."

"Let me guess. You're staying at the Green Meadows?"

"How did you know?" replied Sarah, surprised.

"In our small town there are only two motels, the Green Meadows and the Creekside Inn, and you only stay at that place if your life depends upon it," she laughed.

"You know, we'll be having a ladies get together this Wednesday, and you're welcome to come. It might be nice for our church to get to know you a little bit before the memorial service."

"Let me think about that," Sarah said, knowing she would not attend. "I'll call you if I need anything, okay. Have a good day, Rose."

"Okay, well, thanks for calling. I look forward to meeting you in person."

After lunch, Sarah decided to see Mt. Burney up close. Living most of her adult life in Chicago, it had been years since she had lived in mountainous terrain, so she was eager to explore this environment. She questioned why she had called the church and what she would do in this city for the next few days, so she decided she would at least make an adventure of her short stay by exploring the mountain.

To make it truly exciting, she decided not to use her GPS and to take the back roads, hoping it would lead her to the base of the mountain.

She found Tamarack Road off Highway 299 and turned left. With the mountain ahead she drove forward as the road serpentined through the countryside. At first, she saw nicely kept two-story homes, which she imagined to be from retirees who spent the twilight of their years in this picturesque and relatively inexpensive part of the country. As she continued to drive, however, the road turned to gravel, and she saw beat-up dwellings that looked like shacks. She saw a pit-bull run-up to the chain-linked fence, barking ferociously as she drove by.

As she continued forward, the gravel road dipped, and she scraped the bottom of her car. Further down, she saw names of roads spray-painted on plywood and noticed there weren't any houses around. She briefly considered turning around but was mesmerized by the majesty of the mountain.

She turned down a few more roads and became disoriented. She was not sure how to get back to the main road when up ahead she saw a pick-up truck. It was parked with its tailgate down and a man and woman were standing outside the vehicle, taking in the scenery while sipping coffee.

The man was large. He stood well over six feet, with red, curly hair and a full-sized beard. He wore a large red flannel shirt with jeans and boots. Next to him was a lady, whom she thought was his wife. She was significantly shorter, just a little over five feet. She had short auburn hair, was slightly overweight, and wore a flannel shirt with rain boots that went up to her knees.

Sarah slowly pulled up and rolled down her window. "Hi, I'm visiting the area and am trying to see the mountain up close. I seem to have gotten lost," she smiled.

The man looked at her for a few moments without saying anything. "You're not going to get far in that vehicle, especially this time of year. If you were here during the summer and had a four-wheel-drive truck, you could make it to the summit of the mountain. But with your car and the snowfall already on the mountain, this is as far as you are going to get."

Just then the man's wife spoke. "Hi, my name's Jennifer. This is my husband, Michael. You must be new to the area. How long will you be here?" she asked with a warm smile on her face.

Not wanting to be overly transparent with strangers, Sarah

told the couple she was just driving through and would be in town for a few days.

"Isn't it beautiful country?" asked Jennifer. "I was raised here, and my husband and I decided this would be the ideal place to bring up our family.

"It's quite beautiful," Sarah had to admit. "I just arrived yesterday, and when I was coming down the pass into Burney that home in the middle of the farmland was so charming."

"Yeah," said Jennifer. "That land is owned by the Rathers. They're an elderly couple who've lived there ever since I can remember."

"Yeah, the history of the town's pretty cool," Michael said. "It was in that general area where the Rathers live around 1859 that a group of men was returning from the Pit River Valley where they were snowed in. They came across the slain bodies of Samuel Burney and an Indian boy. A lot of people thought it was a local Native American tribe that had killed them, and they named the area 'The Valley where Burney was killed' to honor what had taken place there. But a few years later it was shortened to Burney."

"Interesting," Sarah replied, as she glanced at the summit of the mountain.

Sarah had satisfied her adventurous spirit for the day and wanted to get back to her motel room to rest. Jennifer, who observed Sarah as she spoke, told her husband that it might be good to help the visitor back to town.

"It was nice meeting you, Sarah," Michael said. "If you ever have the opportunity, head down to Hat Creek. You'll get some of the best tasting rainbow trout that you'll find."

"Thank you," Sarah replied. "I'll keep that in mind."

As they approached Highway 299, Jennifer and Michael

rolled down their window and gestured towards Sarah. "It was nice meeting you. I hope you enjoy your time here."

"Thank you," Sarah replied, as she drove down the road towards Burney.

It was early afternoon when Sarah got back to the Green Meadows Inn. She wanted to know more about the area and places she could visit, so she went to the front desk. She was hoping to find Dorothy, but as she entered, she noticed a man behind the front desk.

"Hey, my name's Sarah Martin. I'm in room six. I'll just be here for a short time and was wondering if you had any recommendations for places I could visit while in town?"

When Sarah had mentioned her name, she noticed a change in the man's facial expression, as if something had just dawned on him. "Is everything alright?" Sarah asked.

"Yes, everything's fine. You said your name's Sarah Martin, right"

"Yes," Sarah replied, wondering what the man would say next.

"I have some items that somebody dropped off for you."

CHAPTER FOUR

Her daddy always got up early and went to the garage to work out. One morning she followed him inside, peeking around the corner while watching his morning workout routine. She watched as he looked in the mirror and let out a primal yell to pump himself up. She jumped, and he noticed her watching. "Sarah, what are you doing?" "I'm sorry dad," she said. "I just wondered what you were up to." "Hey, come inside," he said. "I want to show you something. Come on; do as I do," he said as he flexed his arms. "Now give me the scariest yell you have." She felt funny behaving like this, but her dad looked encouragingly at her. "Honey, you are a powerful girl, and you will someday be a powerful woman. Don't you ever feel ashamed to express yourself and let others know who you truly are."

SARAH STOOD STILL A MOMENT. "HM... THERE'S A PACKAGE for me?"

Who could it be from, she wondered? She had only been in

town for one day. It couldn't have been from Jennifer and Michael. She had only first contacted them earlier that day. As she was still trying to make sense of the situation, the man spoke.

"I'm not sure who they're from. They were here when I started my shift earlier today. I have instructions from Dorothy to give them to you."

He handed Sarah a small box with three yellow carnations. Attached to the box was a card, which read:

Hello Sarah. I hope this gift does not come across too forward. You just arrived and we have never met. Word spreads quickly in these parts. I heard from Rose of your arrival and thought I would reach out and introduce myself. My name is Joy. I was one of your father's closest friends over the last 10 years of his life.

I have included your father's journal. I have never read it, but I know that it had special meaning to him. I thought that you would like to have it. I have included my contact information if you have any questions. Please feel free to reach out to me. I look forward to seeing you at the memorial service this Saturday. God bless, Joy.

She opened the box to see a thick, well-worn leather book. On the cover was embossed the following phrase: *To Thomas, a bold, fearless, confident, and forgiving man. May your journey find you peace and freedom.* Below was an image of the cross along with a passage from Philippians 3: 13-14: *Forgetting what is behind and straining toward what is ahead. I press on toward the goal to win the prize for which God has called me heavenward in Christ Jesus.*

Intrigued, she took the items and went to her room. She set the bouquet of flowers on her dresser, making a mental note to purchase a vase at the local grocery store later that day. She looked at the journal, which had a leather strap to keep it closed, and wondered if she should open it.

It seemed too private, like an invasion of her father's personal space just having it in her possession. Why would Joy give such a personal item to me, she wondered? She again questioned the absurdity of even making the trip as she thought about what she would do next.

She looked out her motel window at Mt. Burney. Dark clouds had formed above it, creating a fresh layer of snow on its peak. She had not noticed it before, but she could barely make out a building on top with a flashing light that penetrated through the cloud coverage like a beacon of hope amid a storm. She stood transfixed by this light and could not pinpoint why this mountain brought about such strange emotions in her.

She again looked at her phone, noticing that she had not received any new text or email. She wandered about the room in silence for the next thirty minutes, contemplating what to do next before finally deciding to open the journal. Not wanting to start on the first page, she randomly opened to a tab positioned at the beginning of the book. On top of the page was listed **Step One: Life Story**, and she began to read:

I had to have been thirty-eight years old. I was a single father of my daughter, Sarah. I think she was in 3rd grade. Nobody at work, not even my closest friends knew, but I would frequent the local bars and invariably hook up with women. Some I knew, but most were strangers. If I had just a little bit of alcohol in me, I was a completely different person. I was the life of the party. Everybody seemed to love me. I was the funniest person in the room. And it didn't matter who they were or what they looked like. It just mattered that I was with them that evening. Sometimes I would bring them home, but more times than not I would either go to a motel or go to their house if their husbands were not around.

It is extremely difficult for me to admit this...I still deeply regret this to this day, but I would leave my daughter alone all night. I do not understand how I could have been so emotionally numb and selfish. I rationalized that Sarah would be asleep and would be okay throughout the night. I thought that the likelihood of anything bad happening was slim. No, that's not true. Honestly, I wasn't thinking of her at all.

This was just one of many indicators of how much my addiction had taken complete control of me. I was willing to sacrifice my daughter's safety for my drug of choice. My addiction truly made my life unmanageable. All I cared about was my fix. I was a negligent dad and continued to be so for many years to come. My actions have caused irrevocable damage to my relationship with others, especially with my daughter...

Without thinking, Sarah flung the book across the room. Startled by her reaction, she took a deep breath, trying to calm herself. After a few moments of pacing back and forth in her motel room, she said, "Who in the hell does he think he is? Like he can just excuse his entire pathetic existence by writing his story in a journal?"

She picked up her phone, searching for any new messages but found none. She quickly scrolled through her contact list, thinking of someone – anyone to call. She found Ron's number, and after a few rings, he answered.

"Hey, honey. What's up? Having a good time?"

"I'm doing okay," Sarah said. "I don't know what the hell I was thinking about coming down here. Why would I spend a week in a place where I don't know anybody? I'm wasting one week of my vacation for what, just to stay cooped up in a motel room?"

There was silence as she imagined Ron considered what to say. Sarah never thought of him as the thoughtful type and was not expecting any meaningful response.

He finally said, "You spent the money and time to go down there. I know you didn't know him, but at least you can get to know a little about him during the trip. Uh…I don't know," he said, slowly formulating his thoughts. "Maybe this is a time when you could reconcile with him."

"Ron, are you drunk? What the hell you talking about? I don't even know why I called. It's none of your business anyway. And besides, you never told me where you were that night when I left the bar. Whose friend's house were you at?"

"Oh c'mon, not again," Ron said. "Look, you're the one who called me. What the hell you yellin' at me for?"

"Whatever, Ron. Look, I gotta go. I'll call you later."

Sitting at the desk in her hotel room, Sarah rubbed her eyes with the palm of her hand. She wandered about the room, occasionally looking at the journal lying partially underneath the nightstand where she had thrown it. What she had read earlier brought about intense feelings of anger and sadness, but she could not get her mind off that book. After a few moments, perhaps out of some desire to punish herself, she again picked it up, continuing another portion of Thomas' life story.

I had always been careful not to get caught with the women I hooked up with. I had done it for so long that I became cocky. I remember it was early morning – about 2:30 a.m. – when I was awoken by the sound of a slamming door. I quickly got out of bed as I heard footsteps coming down the hall. The door swung open and there stood the lady's husband, speechless. It was as if he could not process what he saw.

He was in shock. He did not even look at me. It was as if I weren't there. He then began sobbing while he asked, "Why are you doing this?" He just kept repeating that phrase. That look on his face and the anguish in his voice still haunts me to this day. Then he slammed

*the door and left the house. I glanced at the woman who lay on the
bed crying. She wouldn't look at me either. All I thought of was
myself as I ran out of the room and got in my car. I just wanted to get
the hell out of there. I never saw that woman again.*

*I remember coming home. I went to my daughter's room and
looked inside to see her asleep. She looked so peaceful and innocent. I
never felt so distant and disconnected from her. There she was - this
peaceful, innocent little girl while all I saw in me was this sick,
perverted man. I started crying. I could not stop myself. I had to leave
the room for fear of waking her up.*

*What was I doing with my life? This is not the man I wanted to
be. And I swore I would stop – that I would never do it again. But
inexplicably the next weekend I was in the same bar, following my
same routine – searching for my next conquest...*

Sarah's motel room began to feel like a prison as she
quickly got up and went to her car. She headed to the only
place open late in the evening, the local grocery store. She
didn't care what she looked like. Nobody knew her and she
would only be there a few more days. She walked up and down
the aisles looking for any junk food to make her feel better.

She was in the frozen food section looking for some ice-
cream when she noticed Jennifer on the other side of the aisle
talking excitedly to a friend. The woman seemed so engrossed
in her conversation with her companion that she accidentally
crashed her cart into the end cap of some beauty products,
causing hair gel, combs, and other items to go tumbling to the
ground. She caused quite a raucous, and Sarah used this
opportunity to walk to the checkout stand before she could be
detected.

Just as Sarah thought she was in the clear, she heard a voice
that sounded as if it was magnified by a mega-phone call out,
"Hey Sarah. Is that you?" Embarrassed, Sarah slowly turned

around to face Jennifer, quickly waving her hand to get Jennifer to calm down.

Just then Michael approached Sarah. "Nice to see you again. I know it's a small town, but we didn't know if we'd see you again. How long did you say you would be in town?"

"My flight for Chicago leaves this Sunday."

"You know, you look awfully familiar, doesn't she?" Jennifer said to her husband.

"There was something that stood out in you when we first met by the mountain. What did you say your last name was?" Michael asked.

"Martin. Why do you ask?"

The couple immediately became quiet. Sarah could not understand what the problem could be and asked if everything was okay. Jennifer seemed a little emotional as if holding back tears.

"Thomas is your father?" Jennifer slowly phrased the question.

"Yes," replied Sarah, still not understanding what was taking place.

After a moment, Michael said, "Your father meant a lot to Jennifer and me. His death has been very difficult for us. We're so glad to meet you."

CHAPTER FIVE

Sarah was in a van full of exhausted teenagers who were
traveling home from a mission trip to Mexico. They had spent
the week helping the locals build a church for a small border town
community. She was a natural with children, holding infants, and
teaching the children basic praise songs. The kids adored her. It was
during this trip that she developed a crush on Jake, one of the guys in
her group. They had known each other since they were ten years old
and had not been close leading up to that trip, but somehow their
feelings towards each other started to change. They were inseparable,
insisting on working on the same projects and spending every free
moment together. On the trip home, they held hands as she laid her
head on his shoulder. She had never felt this way about a boy before,
and she held onto him tightly, wishing this moment would never end.

NOT KNOWING WHAT TO SAY OR DO, SARAH LOOKED OVER AT THE
food on the shelves as the three continued to stand next to

each other. Jennifer reached out, giving Sarah a hug, which took her completely off guard.

"Hey," said Jennifer looking over at her husband. "I know you'll just be in town for a few days. How about coming to our house for dinner tomorrow evening?"

Sarah racked her brain, thinking of an excuse not to come, but she couldn't think of anything. "Okay. That sounds great," she said, forcing a smile as she looked into Jennifer's eyes.

"Wonderful," Jennifer said as she squeezed her husband's hand. "Here, give me your phone number. I'll send you my contact information."

"You know," Jennifer said, rapidly processing plans in her head. "Michael and I will be pretty busy throughout the day tomorrow, but the following day our son Nathaniel and I would love to show you some of the beautiful scenery in this area. Is this your first time in Northern California?"

Sarah barely got the word "no" from her lips when Jennifer said, "Well, then you must see Burney Falls. There are so many waterfalls in this area, but Burney Falls is by far the most beautiful!"

"Hey honey," Michael said as he caressed his wife's shoulder. "It's getting late, and I'm sure Sarah would like to be getting back to her motel."

"Oh, okay," she said, glancing at her husband. "No problem. It is late, and I'm sure your tired. Well, have yourself a good night, and I'll call you tomorrow, okay?"

"Alright," Sarah said, happy to be finally leaving.

As she stepped inside room number six, she looked at herself in the mirror. She was exhausted and emotionally drained from the day's events. She took a long hot shower and quickly went to sleep.

That night she had another nightmare, but this time she

was in her childhood church. It was storming outside as she quickly ran to the safety of the building. When she entered, she heard the congregation swaying back and forth to some unknown gospel tune.

She saw old childhood friends sitting next to their families. As she approached each family, pleading for help, they simply ignored her, continuing to sway to the rhythm of the music.

"Will anyone help me?" she shouted at the top of her voice as she stood in front of the congregation. She did not receive a response.

In her desperation, she walked up to the pastor who was directing the choir. "Can you help me? Please help!" As she touched his arm, he turned around and she noticed it was the face of the woman from the dream at the memorial service. The woman stopped directing the choir and stared at her, letting out a hideous laugh.

"Why are you here," she screamed. "You are not welcome here." And the rest of the congregation began to chant, "You were never welcomed here."

When she awoke, she briefly placed her pillow over her face to block out the light, wishing somehow to escape into the darkness. Reaching for her phone, she noticed a missed call from Ron. As she got up, she scanned the room and noticed the vase with the bouquet of flowers that Joy had sent the previous day. She looked at the card, carefully reading the message several times. *I know this book had special meaning, and I thought that you would like to have it*, she continually read.

"This is so strange," Sarah thought. "Why would she give something so personal to someone she has never met?" she kept asking herself.

Part of her wanted to head back to the airport and go back home to a life of certainty. Sure, maybe she was unhappy, but at least that life was familiar and predictable. However, after thinking for a moment, she didn't feel ready to leave. Something deep inside told her that there was more to find out, that she would somehow regret it if she left. Motivated by these feelings, she reached out of her comfort zone and dialed Joy's number.

After a few rings, Sarah heard an older woman's voice on the other end.

"Hello," Joy said.

Sarah was momentarily silent, not knowing what to say.

"Hello," Joy said again, "is anyone there?"

After a brief pause, Sarah said, "Hi, my name's Sarah. I was surprised to find a package from you when I arrived at my motel yesterday."

Joy laughed.

"I'm sorry. I debated for quite some time as to whether or not I should send it to you. I hope I didn't make you uncomfortable."

"No," Sarah lied, not wanting to come across as rude.

"I knew you would be in town for a few days, and I wanted the opportunity of getting to know you before the memorial service. I hope that you are enjoying your stay here."

"It has been eventful, to say the least," replied Sarah. "Just yesterday I met Michael and Jennifer, who said they were good friends with my dad."

"You met Michael and Jennifer? I've known them for a long time, and they were pretty close to Thomas... but we can talk about that at some other time. I was wondering if we could meet in person? I'm retired and have plenty of free time on my hands. It would be nice to get to know you."

Sarah hesitated for a moment, thinking about what she would do.

"Sure," she said slowly, surprising herself that she would agree to this meeting. "I don't know the area, of course. What do you have in mind?"

"Well, as you can see, we live in some beautiful country. How about we go to my place? I can make you some lunch and can show you my property."

"Sure," Sarah said without thinking.

"I'm in town running some errands and can stop by your place in a few hours. How about we meet around noon? You can come with me or follow me in your car if you wish. Whatever you like. I live about 25 minutes outside of town."

"Alright," said Sarah. "I look forward to seeing you."

Sarah spent part of the morning walking down to a local diner and getting a latte, then decided to drive around town. After arriving back at her motel, she was dressing in some nicer clothes when she got a call from Joy who had just arrived at the Green Meadows Inn.

As Sarah walked out the door, Joy was parking her Jeep. For some reason, Sarah was not expecting Joy to be so pretty. She was thin and looked to be very physically active, with a lean and muscular physique. Her long blond hair with gray streaks was neatly French braided. She wore jeans, boots, and a flannel shirt, and she struck Sarah as a tomboy. She was a few inches taller than Sarah with beautiful blue eyes hidden by glasses that lightly tinted in the sun. She approached Sarah to greet her.

"Hi, Sarah. Thank you for calling me. I'm usually not this forward with people, but I didn't want to miss this opportunity to meet you. How are you?"

"I'm doing fine, Joy," Sarah said as she shivered in the cold. She had forgotten to put on her jacket.

After a few moments, Joy stated, "Well, did you want to come with me or take your vehicle?"

"I can take my car if that's okay."

"Not a problem. We can always talk more when we get to my place."

"That sounds good," Sarah said, looking forward to exploring more of the area.

She followed Joy west, outside of town, heading up the pass she had descended days earlier. They continued along Highway 299 another five miles as they approached Big Bend Road.

They made a right onto the road, which was cut into the mountain, with a small, forested canyon to its left that sloped down to rushing waters that beat violently against the rocks. As she looked out onto the valley, she could see the Trinity Alps to the east with snow blanketing their peaks. As they continued forward, Sarah could barely make out Mt. Shasta far off to the North, which quickly became obscured by the trees.

They continued on Big Bend Road a few more miles before slowing down and taking another road to the left. It consisted of dirt and gravel, and Joy opened a green gate with a No Trespassing sign. To her left, Sarah saw a small modular home with smoke that flowed from its chimney. Its yard was full of apple and cherry blossom trees whose white and lightly colored pink flowers covered the landscape. They moved forward, taking a right and drove up a dirt road before reaching a gate. Joy got out to open the fence, waving Sarah forward.

The house looked to be a large two-story log cabin with a circular driveway made up of gravel. There was a propane tank to the side of the house and what appeared to be a garden surrounded by a large wire fence meant to deter the deer. As she got out of her car, she could hear hens nearby, and there was a slight breeze that gently swayed the branches of the trees above them. An older-looking black lab approached her with a slight limp.

"Aww, how are you?" Sarah called out to the dog as she reached out her hand.

"His name's Max. You may have noticed that he walks with a limp. When he was a puppy, he came out running to greet me one day as I was coming home late from work. It was dark, and I couldn't see him. This crazy mutt," Joy said, shaking her head at him, "went right underneath my car. I stopped immediately and looked underneath, and he wasn't moving. I thought I'd killed him."

"That's terrible," Sarah stated as she continued to pet the dog.

"Fortunately, one of the neighbors is a vet, and I rushed him to her house. When I told her what had happened, she couldn't believe that he was alive, let alone able to walk. The only injury he suffered was a broken leg. He still limps to this day, but all I care about is that he survived. I call him my miracle dog," she said fondly, as she called out to Max to head to the garage.

Sarah continued to pet Max, who gave her a single lick on the hand before obeying his master.

"I'm impressed by this place, Joy. You must be happy living here."

"That I am. I like the solitude, but it does get lonely at times. And the winters are not much fun when there is heavy snowfall. Just last year, I had to ask my neighbor to use his tractor to clear a pathway just to get to my mailbox, which is right next to the main road. I think I was snowed in about three days before he was able to help. I guess that as long as you are well supplied it is not too much of a burden."

"Come on in," Joy said as she opened the front door. "Let me show you inside."

As they entered the house, Sarah saw a huge fireplace to her right and a staircase that led to the second floor. To her left was the kitchen, and she could smell the aroma of home-made chicken noodle soup in the crock-pot. There was a brilliant painting of a wave crashing on the surf of a beach as the sun cast beautiful colors through the water. It was mounted on the living room wall next to several shelves neatly filled with books.

What caught Sarah's eye was the large glass window, which faced west. It showed a beautiful landscape of trees and a small hill that overlooked a pond. There were a few dirt pathways and one picnic table that sat near the water.

"You live in such a beautiful place," Sarah said. "I couldn't imagine you ever wanting to leave."

"Well," said Joy, "the country life is not for everyone. For some, the quiet is nice for a day or so, but most of my guests tend to feel restless after a few days. But I'm happy. I can spend all week here alone with my books. Just so long as I keep in contact with my church community, I'm fine."

Both women headed out to the porch.

"So," Sarah asked. "Are there any touristy areas nearby?"

"Absolutely. You couldn't see it, but we passed by Hatchet Creek Falls before we crossed the bridge a few miles back. I would have taken you there, but the water level is so high this time of year, that it is hard to get close to the falls. Maybe sometime this week I can show it to you. It is well-known by the locals."

"If you drive further down the road another twelve miles," Joy continued, "it will take you to the town of Big Bend. It's a small town of about a 100 people or so, with an elementary school and a single gas station. You don't even get cell phone service in the area except by the school. There are many nice people there, of course, but there are plenty of drug problems in the area as well. But the area is well-known for its Hot Springs."

"Awesome. I can't remember the last time I've been to one of those. Sounds like a lot of fun."

As Joy sat in her wooden chair, looking up at the partially hidden sun, she started to laugh. "I remember the time I took a very conservative Christian friend of mine and her daughter to the springs when they came visiting from out of state a few years back."

She looked over at Sarah who sat in a seat next to her.

"I didn't see any cars parked at the entrance, so I thought we had the place to ourselves. We had to have been in one of the baths about ten minutes when out of the woods appeared a naked old man, who walked straight to our tub. I think he was the groundskeeper. He just jumped in as if he were one of the ladies."

Sarah shook her head as she looked at Joy.

"I never saw my friend move so fast as she grabbed her daughter's hand as the two jumped out. She told her daughter to look the other way as we gathered our belongings and left," she said laughing.

"Today, when I have guests who want to visit the springs, I always tell them this story as a warning. With my friends, you never know how they'll respond to public nudity."

As she stretched out her arms and gave a slight yawn, Joy said, "Why don't I make you some matcha tea. It's a favorite of my guest."

"That sounds good," Sarah said as she got up from her chair and rested her arms on the wood-railing of the deck.

She looked at the pond, noticing a small wooden boat floating aimlessly about the water, and noticed the reflection of a flock of birds as they flew above the pond. She could not remember the last time she felt such peace.

"You know," said Joy, breaking Sarah's reverie, as she came out of the house with two cups of tea in her hand. "Your father loved to run. Those dirt trails you see out by the lake stretch out for miles. I would follow your dad on the ATV while he ran. I could never keep up with him on foot. He was too fast. He simply loved to run in nature on dirt trails with me by his side."

"One day he came over to run, and I was not feeling well, so I stayed home as he ran," Joy said as she began to laugh. "He could not have been gone more than fifteen to twenty minutes when he came back all excited. His face was flush red, and he could hardly speak."

"What happened," Sarah said automatically, as she held onto the railing.

"If you were to follow that path up the hill," she said, pointing to the area, "you would come to some power lines, and beyond that section are some densely vegetated areas of the trail. You cannot see more than a few feet ahead of you as the path snakes through the terrain."

As Joy talked about Thomas, Sarah closed her eyes and took a deep breath. She instinctively folded her arms tightly against her chest. There was something about the stories of her dad that made her uncomfortable.

"That day while he was running, he encountered a bear while making a sharp turn on the path. He told me that he instantly froze. He'd left his bear spray at home, so the only thing he knew to do was to remain calm and to stand up as straight as possible, trying to appear big."

"In these parts," Joy said, "we only have black and brown bears, and they are more afraid of you, but Thomas saw two cubs nearby. The momma bear probably didn't want to take any chances and stood up on her hind legs, looking at Thomas. He was certain he would be attacked."

"He just remained calm and didn't move. After a few moments, the bear and her cubs scampered away into the brush. He was momentarily paralyzed with fear before gathering the courage to run back here. He told me that he had never run so fast. Never again did he go out running without me at his side on the ATV."

Sarah let out a faint laugh and a half-hearted smile as she held tightly onto the railing.

As Joy looked out on the scenery, she asked Sarah what she did for a living.

Turning to face Joy, she said, "I work in an Intensive Care Unit in a hospital in Chicago as a nurse. I've been an RN for the last fifteen years, but I've only been in the ICU for the last few years. There's never a dull day."

"I would imagine not."

"Earlier this week," Sarah continued, "a man was admitted to the emergency room who had hopped a freight train. He quickly reached out of the train to recover some cigarettes that came out of his pocket when he lost his balance and fell. He was run over and lost his legs."

"That's terrible. Did he survive?"

"Yeah, but he'd lost a lot of blood the first night, and we didn't know if he would make it. He's very fortunate to have received medical attention as quickly as he did. In my job, you see a lot. Trust me, I've seen much worse."

"I'm sure you have," Joy replied, and both were quiet for a while as they looked out towards the pond, sipping their tea.

"How do you enjoy nursing?" Joy asked.

Sarah gently massaged her shoulder before she replied. "It's all I know. It's the only career I've ever had. It pays well, but it can be very taxing both mentally and physically. It's funny, you know. I've never been asked that."

"Is that so?"

"I really don't know what else I would do?"

"Do you have any hobbies or other interests?" Joy asked.

Sarah looked over at Joy and was silent a moment.

"I enjoy swimming. And I love to teach," she added. "I made sure that my son learned to swim at a young age. I got him into swim lessons when he was only eight. Swimming helped him with his stamina as he got into soccer as a boy. He's very athletic."

Sarah stopped talking and looked out at the trail next to the pond. She took a deep breath, exhaling slowly. Despite the cold outside, she noticed her forehead become sweaty, and she sat down, looking at the brown painted wood on the deck.

"Are you okay, Sarah?"

"I'm...I'm fine, Joy."

"Are you sure? We can go inside if you'd like."

"No, that's okay. I like being outside."

"Well, at least let me get you some more hot tea. I'll be right back."

As Joy went inside, Sarah took deep breaths, exhaling slowly to calm herself.

Joy returned with another cup of matcha tea. She looked at her to make sure she was okay before continuing her story.

"You know, it was about twelve years ago when I first met your dad. With a population of about 3,000 and a congregation of less than a hundred, new people stick out. So, everyone noticed when Thomas first walked in one Sunday morning, sitting in the back. He was so shy."

Joy stopped talking as she looked over at Sarah. She noticed her looking down at the deck as if in deep thought.

"Are you okay? You look like you might be sick."

"I'm so sorry Joy," Sarah said, forcing herself to look at Joy. "You seem like a very nice woman, and I'm glad you invited me today...You have a lovely house." She faltered for a moment. "I'm just not feeling well, and I should be getting home. I'm sorry."

"Pardon me, Sarah, if I said anything to offend you. It definitely was not my intent..."

"No worries," Sarah interrupted. "You didn't do anything wrong. I appreciate you taking the time to reach out to me and to invite me to your home. You spent all this time to make lunch, but I must go. I'm sorry."

"It's alright. There's no need to apologize. I understand. I know that you'll only be in town for a few days, but if you need someone to talk to, I am just a phone call away."

"Thank you," said Sarah, touched by Joy's empathy. She got into her car and headed back to Burney. As she left the driveway, she looked in her rearview mirror and could see Joy standing in the middle of the gravel driveway waving goodbye as Sarah left the property.

As Sarah got back to her motel, all she wanted was to rest. Try as she might, she could not fall asleep. She was restless and didn't know what to do. Nothing sounded interesting to her, so she lay silently on her bed, looking at the ceiling.

She continued in this fashion for another hour before finally forcing herself out of bed. Why was she feeling this way, she wondered? Her behavior at Joy's was completely uncharacteristic of her. She suddenly remembered her dinner with

Michael and Jennifer in just a few hours and briefly thought about canceling. Then she thought what her options would be.

She certainly didn't want to stay in this state of mind for the remainder of the night. Restless and deeply agitated, she turned to her side and saw the journal laying on the coffee table. She felt a sudden urge to throw it in the dumpster but also felt a longing to read it.

She decided to open it towards the end and came to a page titled: *Prayers for Sarah*. She started to read but immediately stopped. Setting the book down, she brought her hands up to her forehead and slid them down her face. She closed her eyes and took a deep breath.

CHAPTER SIX

S arah was sixteen. She was in the pastor's office, sitting alone on the couch. She had never been in this room, and she felt that something was wrong. The youth pastor walked in followed by the pastor. "Hi Sarah," the young man said. "Um," he hesitated as he looked at the ground, "...we found out last week from Rebecca's parents that you are pregnant, is that correct?" Sarah felt devastated and embarrassed as tears began flowing down her cheeks. Claudia and Greg were like parents to her. She trusted them explicitly, and she felt betrayed. "We know that it was Jake," the youth pastor continued after realizing he would not get a response from Sarah. "We tried to reach out to your dad," the head pastor added, "but he hasn't returned our calls." There was silence for a few moments before the youth pastor said, "Sarah, you have been part of this church for the last six years. I have known you since you were a little girl." He was interrupted by Sarah's sobs. She could not control herself.

He looked away from her, pressing his lips tightly together. "I am sorry, but it seems the whole church knows of your pregnancy, and *we have already gotten complaints from some of the parents." Sarah felt confused and angry, but she tightly guarded these emotions. "Sarah," the pastor said. "I am sorry, but after talking to some of the parents and your youth pastor, we feel you shouldn't be part of the youth group for now. We simply cannot condone this behavior, and we are concerned that it would serve as a bad example for the other girls. You are welcome to continue coming to our Sunday services..." She couldn't listen to another word. Sarah quickly got up and ran out of the office, vowing never to step foot inside a church again.*

As she got into her car, she typed in Michael and Jennifer's address into the phone's GPS. Being such a small town, she wasn't surprised that they lived less than 10 minutes away. As she drove through the neighborhood, she saw Christmas lights, inflatable reindeer, and Santa Clauses in front yards in preparation for the Christmas holiday. It appeared to her like any other normal American middle-class city as she looked at the mostly tract homes and used vehicles parked in the streets.

She was greeted at the door by Michael who stated that Jennifer was in her room getting ready. As she entered the house, she smelled the aroma of ground beef, onions, and garlic bread.

"Welcome to our humble abode," Michael greeted her with a smile on his face. "Don't mind the mess," he pointed to the living room. "Our son loves his video games and hasn't yet picked up after himself."

"Hey Nathaniel," Michael called out. "We have a guest. Why don't you come out and introduce yourself?"

A few moments passed before Nathaniel emerged from his

room. He looked at the ground while introducing himself. "Hi, my name is Nate. Nice to meet you," he said, extending his hand.

"Well, it's nice to meet you too. I see you're a big fan of video games," she said, trying to get him to open up.

"Yeah," was the only response he gave. After a few moments of silence, his dad said, "I thought you were going to pick up your mess about an hour ago. Why don't you do that now."

And with a different tone of voice, he addressed Sarah. "Please make yourself comfortable. Jennifer should be out shortly. Would you like anything to drink?"

"I'll have some water."

"How have you liked your stay so far?" he asked.

"It's so beautiful here," Sarah said as she thought about the last few days in Burney. "I cannot get enough of Mt. Burney. I could only imagine seeing that mountain every day."

"I guess like anything," Michael replied, "you get used to it after a while. "I've been to the top of it several times. I even drove my family up with my four-wheel-drive during the summer. There's a fire lookout at the top that was built in the '30s, I believe. It's quite an impressive view from up top. You have a beautiful view of Goose Valley, Bunch Grass, and Big Valley to the east. Too bad you wouldn't be able to reach the summit this time of year with all the snow. Maybe if you come back during the summer you could try then."

Sarah thought it was unlikely she'd return to this area but kept these thoughts to herself.

"If you love mountains," Michael continued, "then you should visit Lassen State Park. It's only about an hour's drive southeast of here. It's pretty awesome. There are volcanic hot springs, geysers, boiling mud pots…"

The more Sarah heard of the region, the more she wanted to explore as she listened to Michael.

"Just last week, Jennifer and I were waiting in line at the store when we overheard a lady who said her grandfather survived the 1914 eruption of Lassen Peak."

Jennifer joined the conversation. "I guess there were a series of eruptions over three years. Supposedly, the lady's grandfather had property on the mountainside, and when he didn't appear two days following the blast, it was thought he'd died. His land was destroyed by the blast, but miraculously, he survived. People thought they'd seen a ghost when he finally appeared, filthy and gaunt from severe dehydration and hunger. According to the granddaughter, he was interviewed for the remainder of his life on the anniversary of the eruption."

Sarah was fascinated by the rich history of the area and was sad she would only be in Burney for a few more days.

"I'm so glad you could make it tonight," Jennifer said. "Imagine the odds of crossing paths with you by the mountain and seeing you again later at the store. Michael and I were talking about it earlier. This encounter must be God-ordained."

Sarah looked off into the living room at the mention of God.

"I know it is a simple meal, but I hope that you like spaghetti," she said. "It's Michael and Nate's favorite."

"Thank you. I appreciate you inviting me over and preparing dinner. That was very kind of you."

"Why don't you sit here," said Michael, as he pulled out a chair for Sarah.

"Michael, can you pray for the meal?" Jennifer asked. The family held hands. Sarah could not remember ever saying grace before a meal, let alone holding hands with strangers, but she did not want to offend her hosts, so she reached out her hands to Nate and Jennifer.

"Lord," Michael began, "thank you so much for providing for the needs of my family. Thank you for giving us life and each other. May we fully embrace our identity in You so that we may bless others in our lives journey. May we truly appreciate this moment because it will never happen again. And thank you for bringing Sarah into our path. Bless her throughout this week and in her return trip home. Bless this food to our bodies. In your name Jesus, Amen."

"Amen," the rest of the family said.

As they began eating, Michael turned to Sarah and asked, "so Sarah, what is it that you do for a living?"

"I'm an ICU nurse at Methodist Hospital in Chicago," she said with a half-hearted smile on her face.

"The Windy City. My wife and I went to Stonington, Maine for our honeymoon and had a four-hour layover in Chicago. We risked missing our connecting flight and walked around the city. It was so beautiful. I've always wanted to see the Sears Tower – oh it's called Willis Tower now - and Buckingham Fountain. You must love living there."

"It's nice I suppose, but after being here for a few days, I would prefer living in Burney. It seems more peaceful. I guess it's like most anything, as you said. The more you're around it, the more you take it for granted. It's probably the same as my career. Every day is different, but I've been doing it for so long that I sometimes get tired of it."

"I understand," Jennifer said. "Michael and I have been teachers for a long time. We know what you mean."

"Are you married, have any children?" Michael asked.

Sarah stared at her plate, twirling her spaghetti with a fork before responding. "No, I've never been married, but I have a son, David, who is twenty-one years old. He lives with his girl-friend about an hour away from me."

Jennifer reached over and quickly massaged the back of her husband's shoulder, giving him a knowing glance.

"Well, Michael and I have lived here for the last six years. I grew up in this community. But when I turned eighteen, I decided to move. I felt that life was too limited here. I wanted to see the world, so I moved across the country to Mishawaka, IN of all places and attended Bethel College on a scholarship where I majored in Education. I wanted to become a teacher, and that is where I met Michael. He was taking the same major."

She looked over at her husband and reached out to hold his hand. After a few moments, she began to laugh as she thought of a story. "I just have to tell you the first time we met."

"Oh no, please don't," Michael said embarrassed.

"Come on honey, we've shared this story hundreds of times. It's so funny." After a momentary pause, she continued.

"The first time I met Michael was at a basketball game. He was part of the basketball team at the college, and he was out on the floor with his teammates warming up before the game." She looked over at her husband who shook his head while looking at his plate of food.

"Moments before the game started, the players took off their warmup pants. When Michael did it, he noticed several teammates laughing at him, including people from the stands. He looked down and noticed that he was missing his basket-ball shorts. The only thing he was wearing was his jock-strap."

"I was so embarrassed," Michael said. "I was running late that day and quickly got dressed so I could join the team for warmups. I remember feeling it was a little draftier than usual," he said smiling.

Without thinking, Sarah let out a snort of laughter. "I'm sorry," she said. "That must have been so embarrassing."

"Yes, it was," Michael responded. "The team and the school never let me forget about it. I was forever labeled as 'jocks' from that moment on. There were less than 2000 students and it seemed that most were in attendance that night."

"Even when I attended my ten-year college reunion, one man came up to me with his daughter and said – I kid you not – 'remember the man I was talking about on the basketball court? Well, there he is.'"

"Are you serious, honey," Jennifer asked. "You never told me that."

"I'm just happy it happened before the advent of the smart-phone," Michael said. "Otherwise, it would forever be memorialized on YouTube for my students and family to see."

Jennifer reached over and rubbed her husband's shoulder. "It was not long after that unforgettable moment that I started to take notice of Michael. We started to talk and became inseparable ever since. It was that same year that I took him to Burney for Christmas break to meet my family."

"Yes," Michael said, "and I clearly remember your uncle not liking me."

"Oh, be quiet, Michael," his wife said, lightly pushing his shoulder.

And then as an aside to Sarah, she said, "my dad passed when I was young, and my mother never remarried, so my uncle basically acted as a dad for me growing up. And yes, Michael, my uncle didn't like any boy I was interested in, but it was a few short years later that we got married in this very town at the First Baptist Church."

"Have you seen the church, Sarah?"

"Yes, I drove by it the first day I arrived, but I haven't been inside."

"Well, then you know how tiny it is. We barely had enough room to fit all the guests. Other than the birth of our son, it was the most unforgettable and significant moment of our lives."

Jennifer again looked over at her husband as they held hands. They gave each other a quick kiss on the lips as Sarah turned her gaze.

Sarah turned to Nathaniel, who was on his second plate of spaghetti.

"So, Nate, how old are you?" Without completely swallowing his food, Nate responded that he was nine.

"I see that you're a big fan of video games," Sarah continued. "I know that when my son was your age that he couldn't get enough of them. Maybe we can play a quick game together before I leave."

"Sure," Nate brightened up. "That would be cool!" Then looking over at his dad he asked, "would that be okay?"

"I'm sure that would be fine," Michael responded, "so long as you finish your food and pick up your room. And if it doesn't get too late, maybe you and Sarah could play a quick game before bedtime."

"So," Michael asked, as they transitioned from the dining room table to the living room. "What are your plans leading up to the Memorial service on Saturday?"

"I'm not sure," Sarah admitted. "It was a last-minute decision to arrive on Tuesday... Oh, I forgot to mention, I met Joy today. She said that she knew you."

"Yes," Michael said. "She was a good friend of your dad's,

and she has some beautiful property up in Montgomery Creek. Have you seen her place?"

"Yes," said Sarah, slightly embarrassed. "I was there earlier today. It's quite beautiful."

"Wow," Jennifer exclaimed. "You certainly have gotten around quite a bit for being here just a few days! How did you meet her?"

Sarah faltered, quickly devising an answer that would omit the diary. "I'd called the church the first day I arrived to confirm information about the memorial service. She left a card and her contact information at the front desk of my motel, so I called her."

"Joy is a retired schoolteacher," Michael stated. "I'm not even sure how long she's lived in the area, but she's been here ever since I remember. She must have invested her money well because she has quite extensive property."

"We've had many Bible studies and mini women's retreats at her property," Joy added. "You may not have seen it, but there are a few small cabins further back on her land."

"Jennifer, you should tell her about the bear spray incident a few years back during one of your retreats."

"Which one?" she asked.

"Remember, inside the cabin?" her husband prompted.

"Oh yeah," she laughed. "Sarah, in these parts it's unlikely you'll encounter bears or mountain lions, but when we go out and walk, we sometimes carry bear spray with us, just in case."

She shook her head and laughed.

"We were having one of our women's retreat on Joy's property, and it was late at night. Most of us had fallen asleep when there was some commotion right outside the cabin. One of the ladies from our group, Martha, was upset because she had cleaned up a mess a bear had made with the thrash earlier that morning. So, without saying anything, she marched to the door with bear spray in hand to scare it off. What she was not expecting was to be within touching distance of the bear as it actually had its butt pressed up against the door while it was rummaging for food."

"She screamed, waking everyone up and instinctively sprayed her spray, getting only a shot at its butt before closing the door. Unfortunately, the bear spray blew back into the cabin, and that woke up everyone, including me. I was exhausted and had just gotten to sleep and was wondering what was going on when my eyes began to water, and I started to cough."

"All of us quickly got up and went outside, gasping for fresh air while we waited for the cabin to air out. And it was so cold outside that night!"

She looked over at her husband who was laughing as well. "Needless to say, Martha was not allowed to carry bear spray for the remainder of the trip."

Sarah put her hands over her mouth, trying not to laugh. "I'm sorry. I'm sure that wasn't fun, but it sure is funny."

"Well, worse things have happened in life. I guess you forgive and forget," Jennifer replied. "It is one of those lessons that I've come to appreciate more as I get older. Besides, Martha didn't mean any harm. It took several women from the group to comfort her as she cried later that night. She was more embarrassed than anything… It's funny how with time you look back and laugh at those events."

Jennifer paused in thought for a moment. "I truly appreciate Joy. She's very well known in our community for her hospitality. She's very special to me."

"Well," said Sarah, feeling slightly guilty at having left

prematurely earlier that day. "It was nice meeting her. Hopefully, I can get to know her better during my stay here."

Over the next ten minutes or so, Sarah sat and admired the pictures of the family on the wall as Michael started a fire in the fireplace, and Jennifer loaded the dishwasher and picked up the kitchen. As Michael and Jennifer finished up their chores, they came into the living room and sat down on the couch.

"So, Sarah," Michael began. "I don't have a background in the medical field. I could imagine that you've seen a lot in your years nursing. Is there anything that has stood out throughout your experience?"

It did not take long for Sarah to remember an incident that took place when she had just started working in a hospital. "Years ago, I was working on the Surgical floor at La Rabida Children's Hospital in Chicago. It was my first time working in a hospital setting. I was working the graveyard shift in the pediatric unit when the paramedics brought in a twelve-month-old who had been severely beaten by the mother's boyfriend." Jennifer flinched when hearing the words but continued to listen.

"It was very disturbing. There was this fragile, chubby little infant with red, curly hair, and we didn't know if he would survive the night. All I can remember is holding him throughout the night as I fed him and sang him lullabies. He survived, but unfortunately, the damage to his brain gave him the characteristics of someone who has Cerebral Palsy."

"Awe, how sad," Jennifer interjected.

"I later found out that an LVN and her husband, a Respiratory Therapists, adopted baby Christopher," Sarah continued.

"Years later I was at a support group meeting with individuals who suffer from disabilities. I believe it was around 2014, about twelve years after the incident had taken place. I was observing the meeting when I saw an adolescent red-haired boy get up and speak. Curious, I asked the coordinators who that boy was, and they told me he had been adopted by Linda and Edward Sterling – the people I'd worked with at the hospital the night Christopher was admitted. His name had changed to John, but I knew who he was."

"What did you do?" Michael asked.

"After getting permission, I approached him and told him that when he was just a fragile, vulnerable baby who came to the hospital that night, that I was the first person to hold and to take care of him." Her voice choked as she spoke.

"I told him that I held him throughout the week and fed and loved him back to health. He became so emotional as I spoke that he started to cry. We hugged each other for the longest time. That was the most memorable experience I had as a nurse." As Sarah ended her story, she looked up to see Jennifer crying.

"Oh, my goodness," Jennifer said, as she dried her eyes with a tissue. "I'm sure you've seen quite a bit as a nurse and that nothing phases you anymore."

"Unfortunately, that's true," Sarah admitted.

"Well," Jennifer said after a few moments, wishing to lighten up the mood. "I need to tell you about an unforgettable and frightening circumstance that took place in our house many years back."

"I'd love to hear it," Sarah said.

After a brief pause, Jennifer began. "One night a few years back, Michael and I were in our room asleep."

"Oh no," Michael interrupted, "I can't believe that you are sharing that story."

"Oh hush, honey. Just let me continue." She took another

breath before saying, "unlike my husband, I typically fall asleep immediately but am a light sleeper. It must have been early in the morning when I heard our bedroom door creak open. I immediately woke up to see a black figure at the end of our bed. I panicked and could hardly speak as I called out asking who was there. I didn't receive a response."

Sarah sat silent, wondering what would happen next.

"In the commotion, I woke up Michael, who saw the same figure."

"My wife's startled voice woke me up immediately," Michael said. "I wasn't fully awake, but I saw a black, large, and silent figure crawling up on our bed. It scared the crap out of me, and I started to hyperventilate. I remember moving my feet as close to my body as possible. Jennifer started to rebuke the figure in the name of Jesus to leave our room, but it just sat there saying nothing. I held on tightly onto my wife's arm, as I gathered up the courage to ask who it was. It felt like my heart was beating out of my chest when I suddenly heard a small voice call out, 'Mummy – daddy…I Nate. I Nate.'

Jennifer's face turned red from laughter as her husband related the story. "My wife quickly turned on the light on the nightstand to see our two-year-old son looking curiously at us from the foot of the bed."

"All I could do was reach out and hold onto my son," Jennifer said, "reassuring him that everything was going to be okay. We both felt so guilty. He seemed to be fine though; thank God. I think Michael and I were more traumatized by the event than he was. We would've never dreamed that it would've been our son! We even let him sleep in bed with us that night."

Sarah's stomach began to hurt as she continued to laugh. She had tears rolling down her eyes. She couldn't remember the last time she had laughed that hard. It felt good to let out so many pent-up emotions since her arrival in town. "That must have been an unforgettable evening," was all she could say.

"You got that right," Jennifer said. "I don't think anyone in our family will ever forget that event."

They sat in silence for a few moments as they listened to the crackling of the fire. As Jennifer got up to make some hot chocolate for the group, Michael said, "you know your dad was quite important to this community. You may not know this, but he started a ministry for feeding the homeless and needy in our city."

"I remember reading that in his obituary," Sarah stated.

"He motivated our church to join him in his cause," Michael continued. "Every Saturday morning, he would invite members of the congregation to go out with him as he passed out food and clothes and talked to people about God."

Sarah's neck tightened as she unconsciously reached up to massage it.

"At first, it was just the three of us, but after a few months, we had about twelve people on our team who regularly met every Saturday at 10:00 a.m. to walk the streets and minister for an hour or so." He paused to stoke the fire.

"He took his ministry seriously. He talked the church board into letting people spend the night in the church when it got too cold outside. It made some members uncomfortable at first, but the congregation got used to it after a while. Your dad was anything but a passive Christian."

Sarah was surprised by this news but kept her emotions to herself. She never thought of her dad as the generous type, but she realized there was probably a lot she did not know about him.

Jennifer came into the room, handing Sarah a cup of hot

chocolate. "Yeah, your dad was pretty important to us. We really got to know him over the last few years. He would come over weekly and have dinner and tell us the craziest stories of his life. We became very close."

"One of the greatest gifts he gave us," Jennifer said as her eyes began to tear, "was how to daily live out our faith through our interactions with people. He was never content with just going to church and professing to be a Christian."

"I guess it will be up to Jennifer and me," Michael said, "to continue his ministry now that Thomas is no longer with us."

"Hum," he said as he stood up. "I know the memorial service will be this Saturday, but maybe it would be good to meet for an hour and walk the streets earlier in the morning. It's something that Thomas would want. You are welcome to come if you would like, Sarah."

She sat silently, processing his request. She was not sure what she would do. Taking a deep breath and letting it out slowly, she said, "Maybe. I'll have to think about it," was all Sarah could say at the moment. They stood in silence, looking at the firelight, sipping their hot chocolate as they heard Nathaniel rummaging through the closet in his room.

"You know," Sarah said. "It is getting late, and I should probably be getting back to my motel."

"Of course," Jennifer said. "Thank you so much for coming this evening. It means a lot to Michael and me. You're welcome here at any time. We consider you part of the family."

"Oh," Jennifer exclaimed, as Sarah was heading to the door. "I just remembered. Michael will be at work tomorrow, but Nathaniel and I will be home. We would love to show you Burney Falls tomorrow if you are up to it."

"That sounds fun. Let me think about it tonight, and I'll get back to you tomorrow morning."

"That sounds fine," Jennifer said. "If you are available, we could go around 1:00 p.m."

"Oh, and I almost forgot," said Sarah. "Tell Nathaniel that I can maybe play that game with him another day."

As she got back to her motel, she noticed that she had turned her phone off. When she turned it back on, she noticed a text from Joy, which stated: *I apologize if I said anything offensive to you earlier today. I appreciate you taking the time to come to my place. It was nice meeting you. I hope you're feeling better. Please feel free to reach out if you need to talk. I am just one phone call away. God Bless!*

CHAPTER SEVEN

S arah was nineteen and celebrating one of her best friend's birthdays from Nursing School. She had also completed a midterm the night before and was hoping to have fun at a local bar with her friends. The bouncers knew they were underage, but the ladies had long ago learned how to flaunt their sexuality to get what they wanted. Sarah was on the floor dancing with one of her friends as the jukebox played their favorite tune. As they danced, an older man in his 30s dressed in a business suit approached and asked the women if he could join them. "Isn't that a wedding ring on your finger?" one of the girls asked. Without hesitating, the man confidently replied, "She's at home and you ladies are here. The night is young. I'm just asking for a dance." The women looked at each other and giggled. After a moment, Sarah approached the man and said, "sure, I'll dance with you." "Sarah," her friends called out. "What are you thinking?" "Don't worry about me. I can take care of myself," she coolly replied. As she swayed back and forth with this stranger to the beat of the music, she never felt so alive.

SARAH WAS EXHAUSTED AS SHE STEPPED INSIDE ROOM NUMBER six. She enjoyed her time with Michael and Jennifer more than she had expected but the day's events left her emotionally drained, and she went straight to bed.

That night she had another dream. It was late, and she was standing outside of Joy's house. All she could hear from the woods beyond the perimeter of the home was the breaking of branches, which became increasingly louder. To her horror, she turned and saw a huge bear emerging from the woods, staring straight at her as it rose on its hind legs. She frantically knocked on the door, desperate to get inside to safety.

Immediately a light turned on in the kitchen. It was Jennifer and Joy drinking hot chocolate while telling each other stories. They laughed so hard that tears came down their cheeks. Sarah continued to bang on the window, pleading for them to let her inside, but it was as if she were not there. They kept laughing, enjoying each other's company, oblivious to the imminent danger she was experiencing.

Sarah quickly glanced behind her, noticing the bear getting increasingly closer. She violently beat against the window, surprised she had not broken it, and disappointed that the two ladies inside would continue to ignore her. She let out a scream as the bear slowly morphed into the same old lady from her previous dreams. The woman stood there, covered in bearskin, laughing at her.

"You see," she hissed. "They don't like you. They don't want you. You cannot trust them. You are not welcome here. You know deep inside that I am right," she laughed. "You will never be welcomed here."

She woke up, sweating, letting out a deep breath. She seldom remembered her dreams, but the vivid imagery and the emotions still lingered in her mind. She felt trapped in her feelings of sadness and hopelessness like a spider's prey caught in its silky web. Feeling vulnerable and alone, she grabbed her phone, wondering who to call when her phone rang.

"Hey Ron," she answered.

"Hey, honey!"

He never used terms of affection. What had gotten into him, Sarah wondered?

"I miss you," he continued.

"Well that's odd," Sarah replied. "You certainly didn't miss me that night you were out with you "friends" and didn't come home. And you certainly didn't miss me the next night when I tried talkin' to you while you were watching the playoffs."

After what seemed like an eternity, he said, "I'm sorry, honey. You know how I am with my sports. I just miss you, okay? The house is not the same without you."

Sarah rolled her eyes and shook her head.

She tended to shy away from needy men. It was a turn off for her. Then she realized she was feeling the same way, which made her feel more confused. "I have to go. I'm meeting up with someone in an hour and need to get ready. I'll talk to you later, okay?"

"Who are you meeting? Is it a guy?"

"You don't need to worry about that, Ron. Besides, you have your "friend's house" you can visit when you get lonely. Look, I gotta go."

She took a short walk outside and had breakfast before coming back to her motel room for a shower. After getting dressed, she again looked at the journal sitting on the nightstand next to her bed. She felt an odd sense of wanting to read more but feeling afraid of what she might find inside.

She looked out the window at Mt. Burney, with white powdery snow on its peak and the barely visible lighthouse on its summit. She did not know why the mountain comforted her, but she suddenly dared to open the book and came across the passage titled: ***Step Four: Character Defects***

I met Jenna at the gym under some pretty embarrassing circumstances. I was lifting weights on the decline bench when I noticed I didn't have the strength to complete my final rep. Suddenly, this petite, 5'2" 100-pound lady came to my rescue, lifting with all her might to help me set the bar back on the rack. All she said afterward was 'be careful, stud. You don't want to hurt yourself.' She winked as she continued with her workout routine. It took me the next 30 minutes to get over my embarrassment and to gather the courage to talk to her, but I knew I had to talk to this woman before I went home. I asked her out that night, and over the next eight months, we became very close.

I had met many women over the years, mostly at bars, but she is the only one I took home to meet my daughter, Sarah. Jenna was special. We worked out together, went on hikes, and even went camping on a few occasions. When I was around her, I felt control over my thoughts. I felt at peace. Being around her made me feel that I was going to be okay. She made me feel happy. My cravings to act out felt under control with her.

She was thoughtful and caring. I had cut my hand on the job and was out of work for nearly four weeks. It was a depressing time for me, but she would come over after work and cook, clean, and talk to me. She would even help Sarah with her homework! She was an incredible woman. She didn't care how depressed I felt; she always had a way of cheering me up. When I felt especially gloomy, she would reach out and tickle me, knowing I was not able to fully defend myself. She was so much fun.

And she always had this sense when something was wrong. If she felt something was bothering me and that I was avoiding her, she would say, "Hey," and have us stop whatever we were doing. And if I couldn't make eye contact, she would gently reach over and touch my face so that I would look her in the eyes. "Let's talk," she would say. "Tell me what's going on?" And she wouldn't let us do anything else until I told her how I felt. Other than my ex-wife, I couldn't remember a woman caring for me that deeply.

Then one afternoon after work, I remember driving home and seeing her walking down the street with another man. I was so jealous. I couldn't stop thinking she was cheating on me. It didn't occur to me to stop and find out what was happening. I just assumed the worst. I didn't say anything to her. I never did when I was hurt.

That Saturday was her birthday, and I had made reservations at her favorite restaurant. I decided to get revenge. Without saying anything to her, I watched as she walked inside, dressed in her favorite outfit with her makeup on. She looked so beautiful. I just waited in my car, imagining her worry when she did not see me. It made me feel in control.

Later that evening I sent a cruel letter stating how I never liked her – that she was of no importance to me. I told her that I was just using her – that I never liked her and that no man would want to be in a relationship with her. How childish I behaved. I was so manipulative. I never told her how I truly felt. I couldn't bring myself to directly confront her regarding that man I saw her with at the park.

When I look back, I realize I only hurt myself. I later found out she was talking to an old friend from high school who had come into town unexpectantly. I never asked her. I never allowed her to explain herself. I just assumed. But the damage had been done and there was no way to undo my actions. She later married and had children. I never spoke with her again. I was an adult man with the maturity level of a 5-year-old boy. What hurts to this day is when I think how she had moved on with her life while I continued in meaningless, self-destructive relationships. Why couldn't I see how special she was? How would our relationship have turned out if I had made better decisions? I will never know...

Sarah looked to the side, burying her chin into her shoulder as she reflected on what she had read. She had not thought of Jenna for many years. She liked her and remembered she was fun to hang out with.

She thought about the time the three were sight-seeing on a boat on the lake. "Oh, c'mon, honey. Why don't you impress us with your balancing skills. Why don't you show us how manly you are," Jenna said, smiling at Thomas.

"Don't 'c'mon, honey' me," Thomas said as he stood up, flexing his biceps and grunting. "This is so easy. Anyone can do this."

The two ladies nodded at each other and rocked the boat, causing Thomas to fly into the water. They gave each other a high-five.

"Oh honey," she said as Thomas doggy paddled in the water. "Does the stud-muffin need some help getting back into the boat"

"Yeah, dad. You're such a stud muffin."

Jenna reached out her hand to help Thomas back into the boat when he pulled her into the water. Sarah jumped in and splashed water on her dad's face.

It was during that same camping trip that Jenna noticed Sarah's love of the water and taught her how to swim. Jenna had been on her university swim team and taught Sarah all four strokes and proper form. It was something that Sarah still appreciated to this day as she swam frequently as an adult. It was a skill that she would later pass down to her son.

Sarah remembered that throughout Jenna and her father's dating relationship that he was a better dad. It was during that period when he and sometimes Jenna would come into her room and read stories to her at night. She was not a little girl anymore, but she appreciated the closeness none the less.

She never knew what had happened to Jenna. Her dad never talked about her again only to say that she had found someone else and had moved on. As Sarah imagined the pain he must have experienced seeing Jenna with another man, her feelings towards her dad began to shift. What were once emotions of apathy were slowly replaced with feelings of sympathy, and it made her uncomfortable. She closed the book, fastening the strap and set it back on the nightstand next to her bed.

She decided to give Jennifer a call. After a few rings, Jennifer picked up the phone. "Hello," she said.

"Hey Jennifer, this is Sarah."

"Hey, Sarah. Good to hear from you.

"I was wondering if you were still up for going to the falls?"

"Of course. I was hoping that you'd call. Nathaniel and I are ready whenever you are." They agreed upon meeting at the Green Meadows Inn at 1:00 p.m.

As the appointed time neared, Sarah looked out her window to see Jennifer and Nathaniel waiting outside in a green minivan. As Sarah walked outside, Jennifer got out of her car and hugged Sarah. "I'm so glad you decided to see the falls with us today," she said with a smile.

It was overcast and looked as if it would be raining soon as they entered the park. During the summertime, the parking lot would have been full of visitors with their cell-phones ready to snap pictures and record videos, but with it being the middle of the week and with the bad weather, they found there were just a few cars in the parking lot.

Starting at one hundred twenty-eight feet at the height of the falls, they slowly descended along a path towards its base. Sarah noticed the intense rumbling of water, which fell from the top of the falls and which also shot out from its horizontal rock layers. The water, a mysterious combination of emerald green and violet blue, violently crashed on the rocks, which quickly moved downstream. Gusts of wind blew through the small ravine, carrying heavy swirls of mist from the waterfall.

Jennifer shouted to Sarah, pointing to rocks that gently sloped down into the pool of water at its base. "You may not imagine it now," she said, "but during the summer, this place is swarming with sightseers who sit on those rocks and take pictures. The water is about forty-nine degrees all year round and during the summer some people brave the cold temperatures and swim even though it's prohibited." Sarah could not imagine anybody courageous enough to swim in that water as she pulled out her camera to record the scenery.

"If we take this other trail," she said, pointing off in the distance, "there's a pathway that will lead you to the top of the falls. There are signs warning you from getting too close to the edge, of course. I have friends who chose to go off the path and ventured too close to take pictures and were heavily fined in the process."

"You won't believe it, but just last year a man walked to the edge of this waterfall and jumped." Sarah looked at the height of the falls and couldn't imagine how anybody in their right mind could possibly do such a thing. "Apparently many bystanders were cheering him on," Jennifer continued, "but after he jumped, he never surfaced. It took a while for the scuba divers to arrive only to find his body trapped underneath some rocks."

Sarah remembered stories she heard as a child of Niagara Falls daredevils who would place themselves in wooden barrels and plunge over the falls. She even remembered hearing of a man who survived the one hundred seventy-five-foot jump off Horseshoe Falls. As a child, she imagined what it would be like to be in complete darkness, trapped inside a wooden barrel, not knowing the exact moment she would go over, and wondering if she would survive the drop.

"So, what do you think of the place, Sarah?"

"Mesmerizing," was all that Sarah could say at first. "I'm in awe of all the natural beauty. I spent part of my early childhood in this part of the country, but I've never been here. I've not seen anything like it, and I love it!"

"I know how you feel, Sarah. That's the same reason Michael and I decided to move back to this area where I grew up. This is where we wanted to raise our son. We prefer a small community where Nathaniel can learn to hunt and fish and to explore nature. This place has its problems like any other, I suppose, but we love this community. We are raising our son where he can see the majesty of God up close through nature. We prefer to live a simple, slower-paced life where we can focus more on family, and we wouldn't want anything else."

She pointed to a bench towards the bottom of the trail. "Just over there," she said, "is where my best friend, Nicole, was proposed to by her future husband. I'm good friends with her then fiancé, and he let me in on the secret. He knew how close I was to her and wanted me to be here to celebrate that event. We live in a close-knit community where friends share in life's experiences. Plus, my family comes down here often. We have camped on these grounds on several occasions and have even fished here at the falls. Sarah, this place is home to me. It runs in my blood. I feel so blessed that my family lives here."

As Jennifer described her life, Sarah felt something was missing in her own. There was stability, happiness, and momentum that Jennifer exuded that Sarah desperately longed for herself.

"I don't want you to think that everything has been perfect for me. Please, don't let looks deceive you," Jennifer said. "There's much more to my personal life than you may know. You just met Michael and me. We've had our ups and downs as in any relationship. The difference for us is that we've been able to learn from our mistakes and have learned to move forward. We've been blessed with a strong support system and have learned to be humble enough to take advice from those who have gone before us in life. Trust me, without help from others, things could have been much different in our marriage. Plus, we share a strong faith."

Perhaps because of Jennifer's openness with her, Sarah felt close and safe around her. She felt instinctively this was the type of woman she wanted to have in her life. She could not remember the last time she had such a strong desire for friendship towards another human being, and she felt a longing to get to know Jennifer at a deeper level.

As they continued to speak, she noticed Nathaniel looking at the waterfall, feeling left out because he was unable to follow what the grown-ups were discussing.

"Hey mom," he said, desirous to join the conversation. "Can you tell Sarah the story of the little girl who got lost from her parents on top of the falls? Please?"

"Oh yes," Jennifer said after a moment. "Sure, I can't believe I'd forgotten about that. This is a story I've been telling

Nathaniel since he was a little boy," she said looking up at the falls.

As her son held onto her hand, she said, "At one time, this land was ruled by the Itsatawi tribe. According to legend," she said, lightly squeezing her son's hand, "one day a little girl had wandered away from her parents and was walking towards the edge of the waterfall. They had called out to her, but she didn't listen to them and had decided to instead go out and explore on her own."

As she spoke, Nathaniel listened intently, eager to hear the next part of the story. "The young girl tripped while walking near the edge of the falls and fell into the pool below."

Sarah looked at the rushing waters as they fell over the falls and thought about the story of the man who had not emerged after willingly jumping and wondered how anyone could survive that plunge.

"The little girl's father," Jennifer continued, "saw his daughter fall and immediately jumped over the edge to save her. He severely injured himself in the attempt but used all the strength he had to keep his daughter above water. Other members of the tribe came to her rescue and brought her safely ashore. Unfortunately, the father was too badly injured and drowned. Instead of trying to save himself, he used what energy he had remaining to keep his daughter alive. They named the waterfall "protector" in memory of the sacrifice the father made for his daughter."

Nathaniel grabbed onto his mother's arms as she had finished, wishing there were more to the story. He had heard the legend countless times and had committed it to memory, but he never tired of hearing it.

This story affected Sarah in ways she could not understand. Unexpectedly, it brought tears to her eyes.

"Hey Sarah, you okay?" Nathaniel asked, noticing Sarah quickly turn her back to him, wiping away her tears.

Jennifer looked over at Sarah as rain began to fall. "You okay?" she asked.

"Oh...I'm fine," Sarah stammered. "I don't know what's gotten into me. I'll be okay," she said as she looked towards the top of the falls.

"Mommy," Nathaniel asked, "is Sarah...."

"Shh," Jennifer quietly told her son. "She's okay."

And then quickly changing the subject, she said, "it's raining. Maybe we should be on our way back home. Hey Nate, would you like to go to your favorite hamburger joint?"

"Alpine Drive Inn?"

"Well, of course," his mother replied. "What other place would I be talking about?" she said with a smile. Then looking over at Sarah, "Would you like to join us? The day is still young."

"Sure," Sarah replied, collecting her thoughts. "That would be great."

Despite the cold outside and it being the middle of the workweek, the restaurant was in full swing, with a line forming outside. The three were lucky to find a booth that opened as a family had just finished their meal. After ordering their food, they sat down to talk.

"Thank you for taking me to the falls," Sarah said as she looked at Nathaniel eating his hamburger.

"It's our pleasure," Jennifer responded. "We've known Thomas for so long that it's like you're part of our family." A faint smile appeared on Sarah's face when she heard this remark.

"Besides," Jennifer continued, "I've never shown up to an unknown place where I didn't know anyone only to reach out to strangers the way you have. That was very brave of you."

Sarah blushed as she took another bite of her hamburger.

"I mean it when I say you're part of our family," Jennifer continued. "I know we just met, but if you need to talk, feel free at any time to call or stop by while you're here. Okay?"

They spent the remainder of their time at the restaurant talking about unforgettable childhood events. Sarah was so engrossed in the conversation that she had lost track of time. She was surprised when she looked at her watch and realized they had been talking for nearly two hours.

It felt so easy to converse with Jennifer. It was as if they had known each other most of their lives. She was thoroughly enjoying herself and was beginning to bond with them. She genuinely loved their time together.

Following the lunch, Jennifer and Nathaniel dropped Sarah off at Green Meadows Inn. "Hey Sarah, thanks so much for coming out with my son and me. It meant a lot," she said looking at Sarah. "You'll only be in town for two more days, but again, feel free to reach out at any time. I only live a few short blocks away."

"Thank you," Sarah said with a half-smile. She watched as the green minivan took a right turn out of the parking lot onto Main Street and disappeared into the distance.

She went straight to her bed and laid down, trying to process the events of the day. She didn't understand how a simple story of a father's sacrifice would affect her in such profound ways. She felt angry and didn't know why. She looked over at her phone and noticed a missed call from Ron. After a few moments of reflection, she decided to send another text to her son, David.

Hi honey. I haven't heard from you. I hope you're doing okay. I've been in Burney for the last few days. You would love it. It has a beautiful 8,000-foot mountain and the most breath-taking waterfall you'll ever see. I hope you're doing okay. I'm sorry for hurting you... She deleted that statement. *I miss you. Please call me. Love, Mom.*

She clicked send, blindly stared at the screen, hoping to receive an immediate response. After a few minutes, she looked to her left at the nightstand and saw the journal lying on top of it. Curious as to what she would find next, she opened it up to a section titled: ***Step Five - Admitted to God the exact natures of my wrongs***

Today has been emotionally draining for me. This has been the most difficult step so far. My sponsor and I sat in chairs about five feet apart as he asked me a series of questions and just let me talk. His first question was: who are you holding resentment towards? I started with my parents. I talked about all the dysfunction and drama I witnessed between them when I was a kid. I remembered the times my dad would push my mom to the ground and beat her up, and my brother and I would jump on his back, screaming at him to leave our mom alone, but he was too strong and would push us away. Or the times we would call the police and they would come to our house late at night. The neighbors came out of their homes, looking at us. It was so embarrassing, but my parents would continue to yell at each other while everyone watched. Then there was the time my mom lost it while I was learning to drive. She grabbed the steering wheel, forcing the car off the road just because I dared challenge her authority.

I especially felt powerless in my relationship with my mom. I could never voice my opinions and tell her how I truly felt. One time, when I wrote a letter sharing my feelings towards her, she read the letter out loud to a guest in our home in the living room in front of me. She laughed and said, 'can you believe my son would talk to me this way? His own mother who has done so much for him?' She was a master at turning others against me. They just laughed at my 'ridiculous' statements. I was so angry that I ran from the room crying.

My sponsor continued to look me in the eye as he asked, 'What part of you was threatened?' I told him that my self-esteem was affected because I didn't feel safe and protected in my home. My emotional security was hurt because I didn't feel heard and understood.

He then asked me where I was to blame. I was offended by this question. I was just a kid. How could it have been my fault? 'It's okay,' he said. 'I'm here for you.' I just want you to learn to take responsibility for your actions even if the motives don't seem clear. 'Just think about it,' he said. "We will get back to this later.'

We met an hour every day over the next week. I went deep into my childhood, discussing the time my 8th-grade girlfriend, Brenda, cheated on me with my best friend. I told him how that incident caused distrust in my friendships and how that event began my hatred towards women. I wrote about the time my sister, Mindy, had seen me picked on by an older kid at school and didn't step in to protect me. Where was she? Why wouldn't my sister help me?

It was such a vulnerable and painful process that it was a miracle from God I didn't act out.

Then one morning, as I went to his house, I noticed that the room looked different. Our chairs were no longer separated but touching each other. He simply said, 'Thomas, I know that being physically close to another person is uncomfortable for you, especially a man, but I need for you to trust me. Sit next to me, please.'

And with my knees slightly separated, he put his knees together, touching my chair. He was in my personal space, and all I wanted to do was leave, but again he asked me to trust him. 'Thomas', he said. 'I need for you to reach out your hands and hold mine.' That was almost too much for me. I felt sick. What the hell was his problem? What were his motivations? He reached out his hands, asking me to *do the same in return. As we held hands, he asked me to look into his eyes. I had never been that close nor looked at anyone in the eyes for that long. Not my daughter, not my ex-wife, not my mother – no one.*

I continually looked to the ground in embarrassment, and when I forced myself to look at him, I could not help laughing. It was so uncomfortable. But he continued to look at me without moving, telling me that it was okay, that he was here for me, that he was listening. He then simply asked, 'Tell me of a time when you did something good in your life?' I was not expecting this question and didn't know what to say. He simply looked at me without saying anything. It then came to me.

I remembered when I was a child and there was a lady from church, Mrs. Terrance whose husband had died. The pastor and another friend tried to comfort her after the church service, but she was inconsolable. She wept bitterly on her friend's shoulder, and it scared me. I asked mom what I could do, but she told me we had to leave the sanctuary immediately.

In our backyard was a garden, and when I got home, I clipped two white roses. I got on my bicycle and rode to the lady's house. I set them on her porch, rang the doorbell, and rode back home before she could see me. Later that afternoon there was a knock on the door. It was Mrs. Terrance, whose eyes were full of tears. She had seen me ride away on my bike and looked down to see the two roses. She told my parents that she was asking God for a sign that He cared and would bring comfort to her when she heard the doorbell ring. She came to me and knelt on her knees and gave me a long hug and a kiss on the forehead. "Thank you for letting me know that God is near," was all she said. Then she left.

My sponsor looked at me, squeezing my hands to let me know he had heard me.

Then after a few moments, he asked again, 'tell me another time when you did something good in your life?' I again reached deep into

82

my memories of childhood. My sister had come home crying after a boy at school had made fun of her. He told her that she was ugly and that nobody would ever like her. I could hear her crying to mom in her room as mother told her that she would be okay. I am not sure what came over me, but I immediately got a baseball bat, and without even knowing who it was that hurt my sister, I marched out of the house to exact revenge on this mean person. My mother and sister went outside to find me and to ask what I was doing. When I told them, my sister reached over and kissed me on the cheek. To this day, that picture of me with the baseball bat marching down the street is safely guarded in a photo album I keep in my closet.

'And how do these memories make you feel?' he asked as he continued to squeeze my hands and look intensely into my eyes. I don't know what came over me as tears streamed down my face and I began to sob uncontrollably. I had never cried this way. Despite all the shit I had shared... all the disgusting, shameful things I had said over the last few weeks, I was overcome with that simple gesture towards Mrs. Terrance and that time I defended my sister's honor. 'Maybe I wasn't such a bad person after all,' was all I could say before another wave of emotion crashed over me, and I again buried my face into his shoulder.

With our hands still locked together, he said. 'No, maybe you are not. You are a giving and deeply caring individual. That is you and always has been. That caring little boy is still inside of you. Despite all the mistakes and hurt you have caused yourself and others, you are still that little boy. Your acting out were symptoms to get needs met from your childhood – to get you back in touch with that little boy inside of you. Thomas, you are going to be okay. Remain open in this journey of recovery. Don't give up.' He paused, looking me straight in the eyes. "I love you. You are a brave and vulnerable man. Please don't ever forget the beautiful person God made you.'

As Sarah closed Thomas' journal, she reached up to her face

and was surprised to feel a tear coming down her cheek. She could only imagine how challenging and courageous it must have been to be that vulnerable with another human being. How would she have responded if she heard another person confess their past transgressions? Would she be accepting? Forgiving? Or would she be critical and judgmental? Did she even have friendships where she could be this open with another individual?

As she reflected on these thoughts, she felt lonely. She thought of her friends at Mic's Pub, and it dawned on her that she was missing true intimacy and closeness with others. The longer she sat alone in her room absorbed in her feelings, the angrier she felt.

Without thinking, she changed into some jogging shorts and threw on her running shoes and headed out the door. It was her first time on foot in the city as she started moving at a brisk pace. It felt cold outside, but she blocked it out. She was in good shape from consistent swimming, so her lungs acclimated quickly to the higher elevation.

As she ran, she thought about the passages she had recently read from her father's journal. *You are that little boy*, she kept hearing repeatedly in her mind. What does that mean? As she continued to run, she reflected on her childhood when she was in third grade.

She and her friend, Jonathan, were walking to school when a group of sixth graders stopped them. They surrounded her and her friend, demanding their lunch money. Sarah instinctively stood in front of Jonathan to protect him, but the boys were too powerful. They pushed her aside and punched her friend in the stomach and took his lunch money. Sarah swung her backpack at one boy, knocking him over when another boy pushed her to the ground. The kids laughed and quickly ran off.

All Sarah could think of at the moment was the safety of her friend. She really wanted to hurt those boys for terrorizing him. She had not thought of this incident for a long time. But as she remembered her caring acts towards Jonathan that evening, she felt she could better relate to her father as that little boy placing the two white roses at the widow's doorstep. Maybe she too was not that bad of a person, she thought.

As she stepped foot back in her motel room, over-heated and covered in sweat, she immediately walked straight to the journal. She could not articulate why, but it was as if the book had an unexplainable power over her, enticing her in to read it so that she could learn more about her dad. Opening the book to another section, she came across a passage titled: ***Step Seven - Removal of shortcomings***

My sponsor invited me to spend the weekend in Newport, a coastal city in Oregon. He has property in the area, and he wanted time in which we could process my step four. He was the most inventive and creative sponsor I ever had. He had this idea of going to the beach. It was November, and it was cold and windy. We only saw a few people that day, an older couple walking their dog. We watched the mighty power of the ocean as water sprayed into the air as it crashed against boulders. I had removed my shoes and rolled up my pants. I liked the feel of the grainy sand and smooth rocks and the ice-cold water as it ran against my skin.

He had me tie my character defects, which I had written on strips of paper, to balloons to be carried out to sea. He knew I still had diffi-culty in grasping the concept of God, so he thought the power of the ocean would serve as a metaphor for the vastness and depth of my Creator's love for me.

It seemed like a silly idea, but I learned at that point to do just about anything he asked of me. I trusted him. I spoke out loud of the time I stole company supplies from work for side-projects to make extra money. I was angry because I felt they were not paying me what I was worth. I wrote the words Self-Justification and Dishonesty and watched as the balloon rose quickly in the air being carried out to sea.

I remembered the time I had an affair with my best friend's wife from work. After our first encounter, she could no longer look me in the eyes. She felt guilty. For me, I didn't care. I never cared. So long as I got what I wanted, I just moved on. I wrote Selfishness and Greed and again watched the balloon rise into the air.

I thought about all the lies I told women in bars. I would say anything they wanted to hear. I always had the same jokes, the same charming stories about how they were different from anyone else. I always exaggerated my accomplishments, painting a false sense of who I was to others so that they would look up to me and respect me. I didn't even know who I was. It was simply a game. They were simply objects for my self-gratification. I wrote Egotism and Denial and watched as the balloon sailed off into the distance.

With each release of a balloon, my sponsor would give me a long hug and tell me how proud he was of me.

I will never forget what he said next. 'Thomas, this process of turning over your character defects to God will be something you will have to do every day for the remainder of your life. Learn to turn over every part of you to God, especially your defects. Do not hold onto anything. If you don't follow this process, you will gradually turn back to your old, well-worn, comfortable ways of coping with life, and you will again be living out of your lack and insecurities instead of as the powerful man God created you to be.

Sarah gently closed the journal as she walked about the room processing what she had just read. Something about the passage reminded her of an incident that took place with her son when he was a boy.

As was their custom, Sarah would read her son a bedtime story every night when he was young. On one particular evening, it was late and past David's time for bed. Sarah turned out the lights in his room and opened the blinds, flooding the room with moonlight. The light cast shadows from the neighboring oak tree whose ghostly branches danced across her son's wall as they were rustled by the wind. David held tightly onto Sarah's favorite teddy bear, Mr. Grumps, that she had as a child as he waited in anticipation for the story to come.

Inspired by the shadowy figures on the wall, Sarah regaled her son with the tale of the magical fairy kingdom whose princess was kidnapped by Ingrid, the evil fox. A swarm of large and angry ants loyal to the fox carried the caged princess on their backs as they led her to the fox's den where she would be imprisoned forever. With the loss of the princess, the fairies slowly lost their ability to fly, so their only way to save her was by jumping from tree to tree as the wind brought their branches together…

At the request of David, Sarah had long ago stopped reading from books as her son preferred to hear stories directly from the imagination of his mother. She developed the love of storytelling in him by saying to her son that all the stories he heard and read throughout his life would be part of his experiences in Heaven. So, the more books he opened up on Earth, the richer and happier his experiences would be in the life to come. David was always fascinated when his mother told him that, and he could not wait to hear the next story she would share with him.

On that particular evening, after she had finished her story, David looked over at his mother and asked about his dad.

"Who's my daddy? Where's he live?" he asked. David was six years old, and this was the first time he had brought up this question.

At first, Sarah didn't know how to respond. Not sure what to say, she simply stated, "he just left, honey."

"Will he come back?" David persisted.

"I don't think so, darling." She did not know what else to say. Suddenly she thought of her boyfriend, Michael. "Why don't you call Michael, daddy?" she asked. "Why can't he be your daddy?"

"I don't like him," was all that David could say. "I don't like any of your friends." He simply put his pillow over his face and turned his back to her.

She had not thought of this incident in years. All she could think of at the moment was why she would tell her son to call a stranger his dad. She felt guilty as she grabbed her phone, looking for any communication from David but found none.

Feeling sorry for herself and wishing to take her mind off her present circumstances, she again went back to her father's journal and opened it. She turned to a passage titled: ***Step Nine - Amends to Dad***

She had never met her grandfather and did not remember her dad ever talking about him. Intrigued, she started to read:

Dad, you have been gone for over 10 years. I can't remember the last time we spoke. Sad to say, I sometimes do not even remember what you look like. I have spent so much energy, so much time being angry and hurt by you. As a child, I could not put into words the feelings your actions caused. As you reached behind the seat while driving and touched my leg, you called it tickling. But I found out as an adult what you were really doing. You would read stories to me at night, making me laugh with your silly voices and then touch me in ways no father should. I didn't know what was happening. I was a child. I was so confused. Despite you telling me that it was a daddy's way of loving his son, I knew that it was wrong. But I didn't know what to say. You were my daddy. What could I do?

And when you would leave for several days, I would go to mom's room and comfort her as she cried. I was only a child. That was not my responsibility. I remember sleeping alone in the living room, waking up wondering where you were. I felt so scared in the dark. I missed you. I needed you. Where were you? My brother and sister and mom needed you. You abandoned us... you abandoned me. I hated you all these years. I wished you were dead.

I am now 61 years old. It took me more than one year in recovery to realize that I grew up to become just like you. The same hatred and regret I have felt towards myself for the hurt I have caused I imagine you to have felt towards yourself. Maybe that is why you left. You were too ashamed to ask for help. Maybe you were too fearful to admit your weakness in front of your family. Maybe you didn't have men and women to lean on who could show you a better path. I don't know. I'll never know. I only know that you are gone and that I can never talk to you again.

I wish you could see the man I have become. You would be proud of the transformation that has taken place in me. If you were here now, I would tell you that I understand you. You did the best you could do with what you had.

I am sorry for not connecting with you later in life. You tried to reach out to me, but I was scared. I was bitter. I was too selfish to look beyond my own hurt. If only I could have told you how desperately I needed you – that I could see past your brokenness and see the beautiful man that God made you. But it is too late.

Dad, there is goodness in every man. I don't care what decisions you made in life. I don't even care if everything you did was completely your fault. It wasn't, of course. Yes, your actions deeply hurt me and our family, and we were never the same. But I forgive *you just as I have learned to forgive myself. I love you, dad. You will always be my daddy. Goodbye.*

Sarah closed the book and placed it on her lap. She sat in silence as she looked out her window, seeing Mt. Burney entirely visible by the full moon with the light from the fire tower shining through the air. She observed its majesty, its stability, its vulnerability, its steadfastness, its dependability, its strength, and without fully realizing why she began to weep uncontrollably.

CHAPTER EIGHT

S arah came home late one evening following a shift at the hospital. Her son, David, was eighteen and was in the middle of packing when she walked upstairs. "What are you doing?" she asked. "What does it look like?" David responded angrily. "I've been wanting to tell you, but you're never home. I found an apartment to move into about an hour outside of town with my girlfriend, Andrea."

"But you're only eighteen. You're just a kid. How are you going to pay the bills?" David looked at her angrily. "Look," he said. "I just got a job at Home Depot, and Andrea is going to be a waitress." He paused, trying to calm himself. "Andrea's pregnant. I didn't want to tell you. I didn't think you would care." "Why would you think that?" Sarah asked, completely taken by surprise by her son's news. "Of course, I care. You're my son."

"Your words mean nothing to me," was all he could say for a moment. "I don't believe you. All you seem to care about are your pathetic male friends you meet at the bar. I'm sick of seeing a different man here every few months. Do you think that is the type of man I want to be for my baby? I may have not had a dad growing up, *but I'm sure as hell not going to follow the example of the men you have chosen. I will be a much better example of a man for my baby."*

"David, you don't have to do this," she said, deeply hurt and desperate to change her son's mind. "I can help. You don't know what you're getting into," Sarah said.

"Look, I'm leaving and that's it," David said. "Maybe we can talk down the road, but I just need space. Leave me alone. I don't want anything to do with you." And with that, he packed up and left the house.

THAT NIGHT SARAH HAD YET ANOTHER NIGHTMARE. SHE WAS that little Native American girl from the legend. Her dad called out to her asking where she was, but she purposely ignored him and walked towards the edge of the falls. She fell and went underwater, barely able to reach the surface before being pulled down again. She looked below, terrified by the sight of her father grabbing onto her leg, pulling her deep into the water. In her confusion, she looked out to the shore, calling for help and saw Jennifer and Joy who walked by, oblivious to her plight.

As she continued to scream out to them, the old lady mysteriously appeared. "You see, nobody cares about you," she laughed. "You have chosen to abandon everyone who has ever tried to help you, and now you are all alone. You have been so ungrateful that nobody wants you," she laughed. "You cannot deny the truth in what I say. Besides, they would just turn on you anyway. Isn't that right?" she laughed. "Look, even your dear father will not save you. He just wants to kill you."

As the woman stopped speaking, Sarah was unable to resist the pull of her father as he dragged her unmercifully underwater. As she looked up, she saw the distorted image of the old woman hovering over her from the surface as she sank to her watery death.

Sarah woke up in a cold sweat. Overwhelmed by the emotions from her dream, she stood and walked about the room. As was her custom, she checked her phone for messages and noticed that she had another missed call from Ron. Annoyed, she set the phone down as she considered what she would do for the day. With the contents of the dream still fresh in her mind, she suddenly thought of an elderly couple with whom she was close to as a young teenager.

Their names were Jean and Frank Forester whom she had befriended at her church when she was a teenager. They were a loving and compassionate couple who took her into their family as if she were their granddaughter. There was the time on her fourteenth birthday when her dad was nowhere to be found. It was a difficult day for her. She was upset and couldn't stop crying. As she headed down the hallway to call Rebecca and share what had happened, the phone rang. She picked it up and was pleasantly surprised to hear Jean, her "grandmother" on the other end of the line. She remembered the conversation as if it had taken place yesterday.

"Hey, Sarah. I've heard from my inner circle that today is a special day for you. Is that correct?"

"Yes," Sarah replied, sheepishly. "It's my birthday."

"Oh, that's right," Jean said. "Well, Happy Birthday, young lady." And after saying those words, both Jean and her husband sang Happy Birthday. "Has anyone told you how special and wonderful you are?"

"No," Sarah replied, as tears rolled down her cheeks. "I guess you're the only one," was all she could say.

"Oh honey," Jean replied. "We're not the only ones who

believe that. Trust me! Anyway, Frank and I just wanted to let you know that you were on our minds today."

"Do you realize that you are one of a few people whom I pray for every day? Did you know that?"

"No," Sarah said as her lips began to quiver.

"My husband and I get up early every morning and we always think of you in our prayers. You're very special to us, young lady! You are a gift that God has brought into our lives, and we want to thank you for all the time you've spent with us."

Overcome with emotion, Sarah couldn't speak.

"Hey, Sarah. We have a special party planned for you today, and we'd love for you to come over. Can we pick you up in one hour"

As she reflected on this incident, Sarah remembered how excited she was as she dressed up in anticipation of her birthday party and how happy she felt when the Foresters finally arrived. What she was not expecting as she entered their house was a loud surprise from her friends who were hiding behind furniture in the living room as she entered. She was overcome with joy as her best friend Rebecca and her friend's parents wished her a Happy Birthday along with other people from her youth group. She couldn't remember feeling so appreciated and loved as she blew out her candles and received many gifts from her "family".

The Foresters were special that way. It was as if they could anticipate her needs and were intentional about being there in her times of need.

Every month she would receive a letter in the mail from Jean who would tell Sarah just how special she was and how God had amazing plans for her life. No matter how depressed or fatalistic Sarah felt about herself, the couple would always challenge her to rethink her circumstances, inspiring her to write the truth about herself on flashcards and tape them throughout her house where she could see and read it aloud every day.

One day as she felt sorry for herself, she told the couple that they could never relate to her as they could not possibly understand her problems. It was that evening when the elderly couple talked to her in their living room. They showed her a picture of their oldest son that hung on the wall.

They mentioned to Sarah when he had graduated from high school and had gone on a long-term mission trip. It was while there that he had fallen in love with a local and was engaged to marry her. Sadly, the two had become sexually involved, and their son had contracted AIDS. When he finally came home, the church gathered around in support, praying for his healing, but within a year he died.

Their son's death took a toll on their marriage, and they blamed each other and God for what had happened to their boy. They had even considered divorce, but with the help of their church community, they were able to ultimately save their marriage.

Sarah had learned an important lesson that evening. No matter what people's lives may look like on the outside, everyone in some form or another has their own pain they are dealing with.

As Sarah continued to reflect on her relationship with the Foresters, she thought back on the circumstances that led her to leave the church. She felt so deeply hurt and betrayed by her removal from her youth group that she stopped all contact with everyone from that community, even her beloved "grand-parents."

They had attempted numerous times to reach out to her,

but she ignored them. Why did she do that, she wondered? They must have passed away long ago she thought as she sat in her room. She missed them and wished she could reach out to the couple.

With these emotions fresh in her mind, she thought back to her last interactions with Joy as she had hastily left her home the other day. She felt the need to reach out to her again. Like Jennifer, Sarah saw kindness and gentleness in Joy, and she wanted to become more intimately acquainted with this woman who had been so close to her father. After carefully deliberating most of the morning on what she should do, she finally picked up her phone and dialed Joy's number.

"Hello?" Joy replied.

"Hi Joy, this is Sarah," she responded, attempting to be as pleasant as possible.

"Sarah. I'm happy to hear from you. I'm sorry if I offended you the other day…".

"It's okay," Sarah interrupted. "I appreciate you reaching out to me since I've arrived here. You have a beautiful place, and that chicken noodle soup smelled really good," Sarah said, trying to change the topic.

"It's a family recipe, which I learned from my mother."

Sarah looked at herself in the mirror, brushing some hair from her eyes. "I was wondering if I may come back to your house again? It would be nice to get to know you better."

"Sure. I don't have much going on this morning outside of a few projects on my property. Would you like to stop by around 11:00 a.m.? I still have plenty of soup left," she laughed.

"Sure. I would like that very much. I'll see you then."

Hours later as she drove up the dirt pathway to Joy's home, Sarah found her working outside in the gated garden. Max, the black lab, came up and greeted her before hobbling off towards the house.

"Sarah, good to see you again. Thanks for stopping by. Why don't you come over here?"

As Sarah approached, she noticed an extension of the driveway that led to other parts of the property. As she entered inside the gate, Joy said, "look over there," she said referring to a pathway that led down to the lake.

"See those ducklings? As soon as they hatched less than one week ago, they immediately followed their mother in a process called imprinting," Joy said. "It's fascinating. I've seen this take place many times since I've lived here. Their very survival depends upon following the example of their mother over the next two months of their lives. Whenever I see that it reminds me of my daughters and how important it is for parents to be strong role-models for their children." As she finished her thought, the last duckling disappeared behind the bush, attempting to catch up with its siblings.

Sarah reflected a moment on what Joy had said before asking a question. "I'm just curious. Could you tell me more about how you met my dad? You've spent so much time with him over the last few years. I'm sure there are a lot of good stories you could share with me. It would be nice to know how you met."

Joy smiled.

"Of course," she said, opening the gate to her garden. "Your dad was a wonderful man and was always good to me. I considered him one of my best friends."

"As I was mentioning the other day while you were here, he was very shy. When he first started attending our church, he would always sit in the back and leave just before the sermon ended. I think it was about two months before he stuck around to talk to the church members."

Sarah stood and listened attentively. She never knew her father to be the shy type and wondered what would have brought about this transformation in him.

"At first, I noticed he wouldn't talk much about himself and would rarely make eye contact. It made me suspicious at first, but after a while, I realized that was his personality. He slowly began to join our weekly Bible studies and became close to certain members of the church and eventually became involved in a leadership position."

"That's right," Sarah said. "Jennifer and Michael told me how he'd started a homeless ministry in the community."

"Yes," Joy replied, smiling. "You've learned quite a bit since you've been here. He took that ministry very seriously and would actively encourage each member of the church to join him in feeding and talking to our homeless population. It made the congregation feel they were living out their faith, not just hearing about it from the pulpit on Sunday."

"That's what Michael and Jennifer had mentioned when I went to their house the other night for dinner."

"Look at you," Joy responded. "You've done an amazing job of meeting people in your short stay in this area. You must be quite the people person at home."

Sarah laughed at Joy's assessment of her. If only she knew, Sarah thought.

Continuing with her story, Joy said, "but it took a long time for him to warm up to me. I remember having only known him a few months when I saw him at the library. I still can't believe this happened," she said. "I called out his name, and would you believe it, he ran away from me," she laughed. "I don't know what got into me, but I actually chased after him, calling out his name. Your father was a good runner, and I couldn't keep up with him. We must have looked so foolish to others who watched us."

Sarah, despite herself, began to laugh, baffled at learning this side of her father's personality. What strange behavior, she thought. But no sooner had she stopped laughing that she felt overcome with a wave of sadness. She looked at Joy's tomatoes in her garden and said nothing.

Joy, who had been working on cleaning up her garden, took off her gloves and faced Sarah. "Are you okay, honey?"

"I'm fine," Sarah lied, trying to gather her emotions. "It has just been a long week for me. I'm looking forward to getting home."

"I'm sure it has been a difficult week for you."

Joy continued to look at her as she decided what to say next. She sensed that Sarah was in a fragile state of mind and didn't want her to abruptly leave again as she had done two days prior. She felt it wise to limit talking about Thomas.

"I'll tell you what," she said. "I have some chicken noodle soup warming in the crockpot. It should be ready. Why don't you come inside with me?" As they entered the house, Sarah noticed the painting on the wall of the beach with the mountain and waterfall in the background. She loved the mixture of colors produced as the light shown through the wave as it crashed upon the beach. "You like that painting?" Joy asked.

"Yes, I remember it from my last visit."

"It was one of my daughter's favorites. It was years ago when she was a teenager when we saw it at an exhibit in San Francisco. She said, 'Mommy, I love that picture. Can we buy it, please?' It was way out of my budget. I was a single mother of two who worked as a teacher, but I would do anything for that girl, so I got it. Both my daughters have long since moved and have their own families, but whenever I see that picture, it always reminds me of her as a little girl."

"Here, come sit down at the table, Sarah. Do you have any children?"

Sarah's face tensed as she interlocked her fingers.

"Yes, his name's David. He's twenty-one years old and has a three-year-old daughter, Kayla. I haven't seen her in a while though. He lives with his girlfriend about an hour from my home..." She trailed off, bringing her hands up to her face to rest her chin.

Again, Joy carefully deliberated on what to say next. She wanted to go deeper with Sarah, so she took the risk of being more personal.

"Sarah. I know we just met, and you strike me as a private person. I respect that, but I notice you're in pain. I imagine this visit has been hard on you. How are you doing?"

As Joy asked the question, Sarah squeezed the palm of her hands together, glancing at the painting in the living room.

"I'm okay," she responded and said nothing more.

Joy sat down at the table across from Sarah.

"Thank you so much for coming out today. It means a lot to me." Then after a few moments of silence, she continued.

"Since our last conversation, a few days back here at my home, it has got me thinking about my life. I've been thinking of my childhood in particular. You may not have noticed from what little you know about me, but I grew up in an emotionally and physically abusive home. My parents – especially my father – berated me, constantly telling me I would never amount to anything. All my parents did was fight. It was such an unpredictable and unstable household. I never knew what to expect. All I knew was I wanted to leave. And when I was only sixteen, I found out I was pregnant. I was scared to tell my parents. They told me my only option was to get married. That's what you did in those days. My father actually officiated the wedding." Sarah looked up at her, surprised.

"We worked hard to make ends meet," Joy continued. "He got work at a local grocery store while I had various part-time jobs, which didn't last long. I spent most of my time watching our two daughters. To make matters worse, we didn't get any financial help from our families. There was so much stress over finances that we fought all the time. I was miserable, but I didn't know what to do. In many ways, I felt as trapped in my marriage as I'd been at home with my parents."

"Then one day, my husband went to work and never came home. He'd apparently developed a relationship with a co-worker and decided to move in with her. I was left alone with my daughters, who were only three and five. I didn't know how we would pay the bills or how I would feed my children. I was just a baby myself. It was the hardest thing I had to do to reach out to my parents for help. I felt so sorry for myself. I felt like a victim. 'Why would God abandon me?' I continually asked. 'What was wrong with me?'"

Sarah listened as Joy spoke, wondering what the purpose was for relating such intimate details of her past.

"But I made something of my life," Joy said. "While living with my parents, I went to school and got a four-year degree in education and later got my teaching credential. I couldn't wait to get out of my parents' house. I wanted to get as far away as possible from that environment and the memory of my ex-husband. I found teaching jobs in different schools but finally settled in Northern California, in Burney. I've lived here ever since."

Sarah stared at the painting in the living room as Joy spoke.

"Twelve years had passed since my husband had left, and I

thought I'd done everything right. I had a career. I went to church. I had friends. I was a Christian. But something was missing. Then one Sunday morning following a sermon, I felt an urge to go to the altar after the service. I don't even remember the pastor's message. All I knew was I was hurting deeply and that I needed to do something with that pain."

"As I knelt, I felt somebody touch my shoulder. I turned to see a young lady, who looked no older than eighteen, who gently caressed my shoulder. I'd never seen her. She just stood beside me, not saying anything as I began to cry. I felt embarrassed and quickly apologized to her, but she just kept gently caressing me."

"It was such a simple gesture, but that kind touch helped to unleash intense emotions of rejection, abandonment, fear, uncertainty, and loss that had been hidden deep in the recesses of my mind. I cannot remember ever feeling so loved and understood as I did at that moment. It was as if somebody saw me at my most vulnerable and completely accepted me for who I was."

As Sarah continued to listen, she struggled with emotions she could not define or fully understand. She had spent so much of her life, especially throughout her career, repressing feelings that she was inept at understanding herself.

At this moment, she wanted to connect, but the thought of opening up to another person frightened her. It was as if her protective barrier was collapsing, and her emotions were beginning to pour out freely, and she tried all the harder to keep them at bay.

"I just met you," Joy continued, "but I feel I know you, Sarah. I can relate to you more than you know. It must have taken so much courage to fly across the country to be here. It was courageous of you to come back to my place after leaving two days ago. Thank you."

"What?" Sarah said, standing up from the table.

"I'm sorry if I came across as rude the first day we met, but I don't appreciate how you're speaking to me now. You don't know me, and you certainly can't relate to me. You have no idea who I am."

As she moved towards her car, she tried hard to keep her emotions in check, but she failed. "I only felt bad because I abruptly left the other day after you spent time making dinner and showing me your property. You give my dad's journal to a stranger... that doesn't make sense."

"You're just a lonely woman who wants attention," she said opening the front door. "You already have two daughters. You're not my mother. Go moralize to somebody who cares. Leave me alone. I should never have come out here," she said as she headed towards her car.

"Sarah, I'm sorry if I offended you. That was the last thing I wanted to do."

Sarah would not respond as she slammed the door shut to her car. Joy put out her hands as if in prayer as she watched Sarah drive away.

As she drove the windy road back towards Burney, she briefly thought about going to the airport but realized she still had her personal belongings in her motel room. Deeply agitated, she yelled out, "Who in the hell does she think she is? She doesn't know me. Why in the hell did I ever come here?"

She rushed back to her motel room and decided to take a shower to calm herself. As she dressed, she again considered gathering her belongings and heading to the airport before noticing the leather-bound journal with the black embossed print on its cover lying at its usual spot on the nightstand next to her bed.

She again looked out the window at the mountain and suddenly felt at peace. She didn't understand the odd relationship she had with the mountain, but it always seemed to put her at ease. As she laid down on her bed, absorbed in feelings of self-pity and loneliness, she opened the journal to another entry labeled: *Service*

It was a difficult day. I felt alone and sorry for myself. I didn't have anyone to talk to. My mind kept racing back to all the mistakes I had made, telling me what a loser I was. I felt out of my mind with anxiety, and all I wanted to do was to act out. I hate it when I felt trapped by these feelings. My sponsor must have also hated these feelings because when I called him this time, he had a new challenge for me.

After only talking to him one minute, he cut me off and asked a question. 'Do you want to live in the problem or the solution?' Pissed that he had cut me off, I annoyingly said, 'solution, of course.'

'Okay,' he said casually. 'Why don't you do this then. Get a piece of paper and write at least 10 ways in which you can be of service to someone and call me back when you have done so.' And before I could say anything, he HUNG UP ON ME!

What the hell is his problem? Who does he think he is? For the next two minutes, I was seething in anger at his disrespect and called him back. The first words that came from his mouth when he answered the phone were: 'Did you complete the assignment?'

'No,' I stammered out, but before I could say anything else, he hung up on me again! That son-of-a-bitch, I yelled. I spent the next five minutes pacing my room, shouting in anger until I felt myself calm down. Then after my irritation subsided, I thought I could at least try to create a list. It wasn't much. I had no idea what I could do. 1) Pick up trash at the park. 2) Visit a local church and see if they

*needed any help. 3) Clean parking lot of apartment complex nearby.
4) Help an elderly woman bring her groceries to her car. 5) Adopt a
starving child in Africa and raise him to be a world-leader (alright, so
maybe I was still a little pissed by the assignment.)*

*I finally called my sponsor with my complete list, and he chal-
lenged me to put into action one of those steps just for today and then
hung up on me again. Annoyed, I looked at my list and thought about
what I would do. I reasoned that picking up a few pieces of trash at
the apartment complex down the street would be the least inconve-
nient as I headed out the door.*

*It felt so freaking embarrassing. Who in their right mind on their
day off (or any day of the week for that matter) walks around picking
up trash? I imagined everyone in the apartment complex locking
their doors, keeping their children close, wondering what this crazy
man was up to. Nobody simply helps others unless there is something
in it for them.*

*Then a car drove into the parking lot and parked next to where I
was picking up trash. An elderly woman slowly got out of her car,
eyeing me carefully as she did so. I walked in her direction and she
immediately shut her door and locked it.*

*Who in the hell did she think I was? Some perverted, desperate
maniacal serial killer who preyed on helpless elderly women in broad
daylight to get his kicks? I was already uncomfortable enough as I
walked to another part of the parking lot, hoping to finish up my
good deed for the day so I could go home.*

*Would you know it, not 10 minutes had elapsed when the police
arrived. They got out of their car and said that there were a few calls
of suspicious behavior from a man who matched my description: as if
picking up trash was akin to peeking through people's windows or
breaking into their cars. They asked me if I had lived there and what
I was doing? What the hell was I supposed to tell them? That I had
intense cravings of acting out and that my sponsor challenged me to*

make a list of ways to relieve my pent-up feelings? What the hell was that old woman's problem I thought as I spoke with the officers.

They ran my driver's license as if they suspected I was a felon who had broken out of prison. After a brief explanation that I was simply a Good Samaritan who was trying to help clean up the community, the officers finally let me go. After all of that, one of the officers eyed me suspiciously as if to say that he still did not quite believe me and would be keeping careful watch over me. What a wonderful introduction to the concept of giving. With these types of experiences, I cannot wait for the next time to be of service to my fellow human being.

Despite her feelings of self-pity, Sarah could not help but laugh. The thought of an elderly woman scared for her life and the police questioning her dad was too much. Whatever journey it was that her dad had undertaken, it seemed to have radically changed him, she had to admit.

As she thought about the theme of giving, she reflected on one of her trips to Mexico with her youth group. Sarah had befriended a Mexican girl in the community they were serving. Her name was Laura, and her new friend followed her everywhere. Despite the language barrier, they communicated well. Sarah taught her a few praise songs and even showed her how to make her favorite breakfast: scrambled eggs with skillet fried potatoes.

The girl showed Sarah her favorite doll, a Raggedy Ann that was filthy from spending time outside in the dirt. Sarah took compassion on her and spent time playing games with her, such as hide and go seek and house. The youth group leader jokingly said that she had found her long lost sister.

The last day of the trip was especially difficult for Sarah as she had to say her goodbyes. Laura was crying as she reached out her hands to give Sarah her doll. Sarah tried to refuse the gift, but Laura insisted that she have it. As Sarah took hold of it, she wrapped her arms around the girl, not wanting to let go.

As the van drove away, Sarah looked back to see Laura waving goodbye as both girls continued to cry. As the youth slept in the van on their way home, Sarah held the doll close to her body, wondering if she would ever see Laura again.

As Sarah thought back on this incident, she wondered what had happened to that the doll, and thought about how meaningful it was for Laura to have given it to her. She did not expect this memory to be so emotional as she began to presently cry. When was the last time she had given her time, money, or services to another, she wondered? Who were the Laura's in her community that she could reach out to?

As she continued immersed in these feelings, she looked again at her father's journal. Hoping to learn more about him, she opened it to another tab, which read: **Step Eleven – Knowledge of His will**

God, I was walking down the street today when a homeless man approached me asking for money. This sort of thing happens all the time. I usually get annoyed and ignore the person, but something different took place inside of me today. I remember a passage from the sermon I had heard the week before that stated: 'Truly I tell you, whatever you did for one of the least of these brothers and sisters of mine, you did for me.' The pastor said that when you give to the needy you are giving to the Lord. I felt convicted.

For the first time in my life, I turned around and gave the coat off my back to a stranger. I think the man was more surprised than me. I talked to him for a few minutes. His name was Matthew, and he was in the Vietnam war. He had two adult children whom he had not seen in years. I felt such compassion for this man. The more I talked to him, Father, the more connected I felt with you.

An idea formed in my head. I feel that you have called me to help feed and clothe the homeless in Burney. I have never felt so convicted and in line with your will. Thank you so much, God, for helping me to find part of my purpose in my life. Amen.

Sarah slowly closed the journal. This was so unlike the man she had known – or thought she had known- growing up. She had this nagging question in her mind, which she needed to be answered. Desperate, she uncharacteristically drove to Jennifer and Michael's house without calling first. It was the middle of the day, and she was not sure if they would be home.

As she knocked on the door, part of her hoped that nobody would answer.

"Oh, hey Sarah. I was not expecting you. Would you like to come in?"

Sarah faintly smiled, avoiding eye contact with Jennifer.

"Are you okay?" Jennifer asked. "Here, c'mon inside," she said, hugging Sarah. "Michael and Nathaniel are off hiking in the woods. They try to do at least one activity together weekly. It's their father and son time. Would you like something to drink?"

"That's okay," Sarah said. "I guess I have a lot on my mind since coming here."

"That makes sense to me. You just found out your father died. You are in a new place meeting new people. There is a lot for you to process...."

She stopped as she noticed Sarah glance down at the carpet. "What's wrong?"

"I don't know," Sarah responded as she brushed her right foot against the carpet. "Is it possible for somebody to change?" She paused, thinking on how to expand upon the question. "I mean, can a person who has destroyed their life become somebody different? Or will they always be subject to their impulses and base nature?"

There were a few moments of silence as Jennifer pondered the question. Before she could respond, Sarah suddenly got up to leave, feeling embarrassed by her frankness with Jennifer. "Hey Sarah, please, sit down. It's okay. I'm glad you came. There's nothing wrong with opening up with me. I'm a safe person."

She looked Sarah in the eyes, considering what she would say next before responding. "I'm glad you came. I appreciate how you must feel. Michael and I are very private people as well. There are things about us only a few trusted people know. To answer your question, I want to share something very personal with you. I trust you will keep it private."

"Sure," Sarah said as she leaned back on the couch.

"Michael and I experienced some difficulties in our marriage about a year ago. You don't know this, but I was an English teacher at Burney High School. I worked there for seven years and loved my students. Unfortunately, I started to become close to another faculty member. He was a mathematics instructor, and at first, we talked about how we would work together to help a few troubled students we shared. What started as an innocent, work-related chat eventually became deeper. Over time we began talking about issues regarding our marriages."

"His wife had a miscarriage and was emotionally distant from him. Michael was spending a lot of time in his work and with his friends and was becoming increasingly distant from me. That man listened and paid attention to me in ways Michael hadn't done since the beginning of our marriage. He was meeting my needs of being known and cared for. At least that's what I told myself. I was in denial. I knew we were heading down a wrong path, but part of me didn't want for it to stop, and I didn't have anyone to open up to."

"When I look back on those events, I knew deep inside that I had choices, but I fooled myself into believing that what I eventually chose was the only course open to me. I kept the ensuing affair a secret from everyone. I was miserable."

"Unfortunately, the man's wife found out. Understandably, she was extremely upset and sent a very explicit and embarrassing email to the principal. I was brought into the office to answer for my actions. It was a painful process for me, but I decided for a time I would take a leave from teaching to focus on my family life. Michael was devastated. He'd be gone for days, and when he did come home, he would completely ignore me."

"Nathaniel felt especially hurt by the tension in the household. He took his father's absence personally, thinking it was because of him. There were so many questions he had, but Michael and I didn't know how to respond. We both grew up with parents who stayed together. This was new territory for us. We didn't feel comfortable reaching out to our church family. We were scared we would be judged and ostracized."

"Then one evening, about a month after the disclosure of the affair, I was reading a book in bed when Michael suddenly entered the room. He walked over to me and knelt on his knees, burying his face into my lap. This large, powerful man, whom I had never seen that vulnerable, started to cry as he asked forgiveness for his behavior. I couldn't believe what he'd just asked. It broke me. 'Forgive you? I'm the one who needs to be forgiven for my actions towards you,' I said.

'Honey,' he told me. 'I've failed in my duty as both a husband and a father. I made my work and friendships a higher priority than our marriage. I can think of some of the times you tried to reach out to me, and I would ignore you. I took our relationship for granted. I didn't give you the love and attention you deserved.' And my husband again looked up at me with tears rolling down his cheeks, and he said, 'Your actions have deeply wounded me. I've never been so hurt and felt so betrayed in my life.'

As Jennifer continued to speak, she began to choke up and had to pause to gather her emotions. When she was able to recover, she said, "my husband told me, 'Jennifer. I forgive you. I don't hold against you any past decisions you've made that hurt our marriage. In fact, I choose not to hold against you any decision you may make in the future regarding our marriage. No matter what happens, I love you unconditionally.'

Tears now came down Jennifer's cheeks as she related the story. 'It's for you to decide if you wish to keep in connection with me," she continued to relate what her husband had told her that evening. "It's up to you if you want to preserve our marriage. Regardless of what you decide, I will always – no matter what – love you. I've made my choice. I choose you.'

Jennifer briefly stopped speaking as she looked Sarah straight in the eyes.

"Sarah, everything that happened that evening – the culmination of my husband's speech – his dramatic change in the outlook on our marriage - was a direct result of your father. Sarah, your father helped Michael to process his emotions of betrayal, hurt, and disappointment. If it weren't for Thomas, I'm afraid we wouldn't be married today. He challenged Michael to rethink how he perceived my infidelity by using it as a catalyst for becoming a better man."

"Your father was our most valued and trusted friend. He taught Michael how to be a husband – how to forgive and to unconditionally love his wife. He taught me how to forgive myself and how to reconcile with my husband."

She paused again for a moment to allow her emotions to calm.

"So, to answer your question, can people change? Yes, both Michael and I are living testaments that human beings are not the products of their past choices. They can change. It may be harder for some than for others, but it's in large part the meaning we give our circumstances that allows us to make positive choices in our lives. We don't have to be victims. There's always hope."

Jennifer reached out to hug her friend, but Sarah moved away from her.

"I'm sorry, Jennifer. Don't take offense."

"It's okay, Sarah."

"Thanks for opening up to me. I just need to be alone. I think I should go."

"I understand," Jennifer said. "I respect your space. I know the memorial service is tomorrow and that you'll be leaving soon. You're welcome to call and come over at any time. I choose to stay in connection with you, Sarah. I love you."

"Thank you," Sarah said, as she got in her car and drove back to her motel.

CHAPTER NINE

Thomas came home late from work. It was dark outside and all the lights in the house were out. The only light he could see came from the garage. Concerned, he walked inside. As he entered, he noticed that all his neatly placed tools where strew about the place as if someone had broken in. His 1970 yellow Dodge Charger, his most prized possession, which he always kept covered, was severely scratched on its hood and passenger side door. The windshield had a crack in it as if someone had hit it with a baseball bat. He saw a hand-written letter on his workbench, which read: I hate you. I hope to never see you again so long as you live. You are a pathetic excuse for a father. And so long as I live, you will never get to know your grandson.

SARAH TRUDGED INTO ROOM SIX AT GREEN MEADOWS INN, overwhelmed by exhaustion and emotion. She would be leaving in less than forty-eight hours, but something was compelling her to keep reading the journal. She had to know more. She needed to get to know this man Jennifer credited for radically changing her marriage. There were so many questions. Maybe the unread pages of the journal had the answers. As she moved towards the end of her father's writings, she came across a section titled: **Step Twelve** - *Carrying the message to others*

I felt I experienced a break-through today while walking the streets and ministering to the homeless. I was at Bailey Park with my group. It consists mostly of church members, but we even have a few of the homeless who join us every Saturday. There is something powerful when one drug addict or alcoholic can confront another, especially someone they know and share with them how their life has changed.

Just today at the park I encountered Dwayne. He is an extremely angry and volatile man. I found out from others his daughter died of a drug overdose, and he felt responsible for getting her started. Our group tried so many times to reach out to him, but he would throw things and cuss us out. He would constantly shout: 'We don't want your handouts. Take your God-damned religion back to the church where it belongs.' We usually stayed clear of him, but something inside prompted me to talk to him.

I was nervous as I approached. He kept yelling at me to leave him alone and that he would hurt me if I got too close. I just kept my arms out and slowly walked towards him as others in the group prayed. I felt God telling me that this man needed my help. I was afraid as I approached him. 'Hey, Dwayne, what's wrong?' I said. 'Don't pretend you know me,' he responded. 'You talk about God and how he changes people. Your God is worthless. Fairy-tale; wishful thinking. Your religion means shit.'

Keeping my arms out as I continued to move closer, I simply said I knew he was in pain. I didn't know what his beliefs in God were, and it didn't matter to me. All I knew was he was in pain and that I loved him. And just like that something changed in this man. He started to cry. I didn't think it was possible, but I reached out and hugged him.

He smelled so terrible, but it didn't matter. I felt the love of God flowing through my veins as I told him that no matter what he had done that I would always love him – that God would always love him. I told him about all the people I had hurt – the relationships that would never be mended. I had to learn how to forgive myself. He could too.

I will try to reach out to Dwayne again this Wednesday. I love that man. I just want to connect with these men and women You have brought in my path. Their pain and regret have destroyed their lives. They have lost so much. I know how they feel because I am one of them. God, thank you for this ministry. It is one of the most challenging yet meaningful things I have ever done. Please do not let my endeavors be in vain. I want to see you work through me to change the lives of these people. Amen.

Sarah suddenly heard her phone ring. Thinking it was perhaps Joy or Jennifer, she looked at the screen and noticed an incoming call from Ron. A few days earlier she would have been happy to have heard from him, but something had changed in her brief few days in Burney. She felt she had more important matters to think about as she turned the phone off so she would not be interrupted.

She felt oddly fascinated by this side of her dad. A man who she barely knew growing up, who only seemed to care about himself, had somehow transformed himself. How? She could not make sense of the prayer from his last journal entry. He found God? She scoffed. No, that could not be, she thought. He must have been delusional. He must have been in denial.

How else could a man who made fun of her for going to

church, who said that if she wished to believe in fairy tales that she should just keep them to herself, have suddenly given his life to God? No. He was simply manipulating others.

He wanted to hide behind his religion so that people would only see what he wanted them to see. Yes, she thought. That was the only reason he could have befriended people like Joy, Michael, or Jennifer. They simply didn't know who he truly was. Only she knew his true self. She laughed and closed the book.

It was late, and she knew she would be leaving soon. Despite her exhaustion, she didn't want to go to bed. Restless, she decided to drive around town. She felt compelled to take the journal with her as she left her room.

It was around 8:00 p.m., and it was dark outside. It was a cold, clear night with a full moon. Off in the distance, she saw the light originating from the fire-watch tower on the top of Mt. Burney as she drove down the main road. She saw the town's movie theater that played only one movie for just two showings per day. Most businesses had already closed, but the town's single grocery store was still open.

She saw a few cars in the parking lot and saw two people conversing and smoking cigarettes as she drove by. Impulsively, she felt the need to drive to the park her dad had mentioned in the journal entry. Not knowing where she was going, she made a right-hand turn and followed the road a few blocks before seeing a sign for Bailey Park.

As she approached it, she reflected on her father's journal entry. She imagined a pathetic group of elders from a church that nobody cared for walking around handing out food and blankets to people who probably feigned interest just for the free items. Yet she got out of her car and put on her jacket as she approached the park's entrance. Not wanting to walk alone inside the park late at night, she stayed in the parking lot under a streetlight.

"Who were you, Thomas?" she asked. "Why would you approach a homeless man who threatened to harm you and then hug him? That doesn't make sense. What were you doing befriending a couple of half your age and giving them marriage advice? You of all people. What in the hell did you know about marriage? You never had one healthy relationship in your pathetic life, not even with my mother," she said as the light showed her breath from the cold air. As she continued to talk, she became angrier. The quietness and aloneness of the night gave her the courage to vent her emotions openly.

"How in the hell did you become close with Joy? She must not have known you. If she did... if she had any sense, she would have left you like every other woman in your life. You're a loser," she shouted. She waited in silence as if expecting a response from her deceased father.

Frustrated, she got into her car, aimlessly traveling down one road after another, not caring where she ended up. Immersed in her feelings, she didn't notice a car up ahead that was at a complete stop. She slammed on her brakes, scaring the individual in front of her, who quickly moved forward. In the commotion, her father's journal fell to the floorboard. As she looked up, thankful that she had not gotten in an accident, she saw in the distance the steeple of a church and a solitary tree whose branch swung back and forth in the wind above it.

In front of the building was an old lit sign which read, "First Baptist Church". How did she end up here, she asked herself? She pulled over her car on the other side of the street, not daring to enter the parking lot.

She saw the journal lying on the floorboard of the passenger seat. She quickly picked it up and saw it was open to a passage titled: *Turn my will over to God.* "How convenient," she laughed. "God, after all these years, are you now ready to talk to me?" she mocked. She almost expected a response but felt even angrier when she received none.

She did not want to leave just yet and continued parked on the side of the road. In the distance, she could see the light protruding through the cloud coverage on the top of Mt. Burney.

Looking at the building gave her an intense feeling of loneliness and pain yet also an odd sense of hope. She could not make sense of her feelings, and the only thing she knew was to remain parked along the side of the road, somehow hoping that the church would provide answers her soul longed to hear. After a moment's pause, she picked up the journal, turning on the interior light so she could read. Squinting, she read the following passage: ***Step Two – Belief in Higher Power***

It is one thing to admit that I have a problem I cannot solve, that I am powerless. I had to get up in front of a group of friends and strangers and share my whole life story with them. It was a humbling experience, but it was a powerful step in my recovery process. But it is another thing altogether to accept that my only hope for freedom – for a new life is through trusting in God. Whose God? What has He/She/It ever done for me? Is He the God of my childhood? The God of my parents who pretended to believe in Him on Sundays to impress their friends only to reveal their true selves to us kids in the privacy of our home? The same God who my father claimed disciplined those He loved as he beat us and mom mercilessly for the smallest sign of disrespect. Where was God when I was left alone as a child? What happened to Him when our mom left, and my dad was seldom at home? God? That God? Or the God who let my 16-year-old brother, Tim, die in a car accident when he was only a child? He had his whole life ahead of him. It destroyed our family. That is the God that I must now put my faith in? Now he is suddenly going to love and help me? Now he will miraculously show up? It does not make sense. Religion, the cross, sacrificing God's son, none of it makes any sense. Christianity does not make sense. It has never helped me, and I fail to understand how it will help me now.

Sarah stopped reading for a moment as she rolled down her window and looked over at the church. She knew very little about her uncle, Tim. Her father never talked about him, and she had no idea he had passed. What other secrets were there in her family? Despite her anger, she felt a moment of pity for the pain she imagined her dad to have experienced at such a young age.

She also had not known of her dad's mother leaving the family either when he was a teenager. As she reflected on her grandmother's funeral and the comments her aunt had made towards her dad, she felt a deeper connection with him. She continued to read.

Then there was my wife and my daughter. I haven't spoken to my daughter in years. I can't blame it all on God. I know much of it is my fault. But it is hard for me to believe that there is something – anything out there that is bigger than me that would love me and help me to do what I cannot do for myself. And then there is the question of how to define God. Some would argue that I should let go of the God of my childhood and define my own Higher Power. According to them, each person has an understanding of God that is personalized for them. Some feel that the collective wisdom in the group is their Higher Power while others use powerful forces of nature as their God. I don't know what to believe. It is all so confusing to me.

My sponsor asked me a powerful question that I have not been able to forget to this day. He simply asked me to write the attributes of a Higher Power that I could put my trust in. I got to choose how I viewed God? It seemed so blasphemous; it seemed too simple. It took me forever to write these qualities, but it seemed as if I had always known them.

I wrote that I needed a God who was Gentle, Trusting, Merciful, Forgiving, Dependable, Loving, Giving... I could not even complete the list when I started to cry as I had never done before. At that moment, the presence of God had never felt so powerful. It was as if my Higher Power were beside me, embracing me as He told me that everything would be okay – that he would be there for me.

God, I said. Whoever you are, I am willing to do whatever it takes to get better. If that means believing in you, I will do it. I still don't know if I am just talking to myself or if you truly exist, but I am willing to believe. God, help me to believe. It is all that my sponsor has required of me, to be willing. And I am ready to do whatever he asks of me... I believe You exist. Make yourself known to me, God...As the Big Book says, 'do with me as Thou wilt'. Amen.

Sarah stared at the passage in silence, meditating on what she had read. She had not thought much about the concept of God since high school. She was a child then. That was a lifetime ago. Through her time in school and her nursing career, she had lost whatever faith remained. She again looked at the building across the street, with a beautiful stained-glass image of the cross built into the front of the structure.

She looked over to the mountain, imagining the powerful forces in the earth that helped shape it, and considered the possibility of God. Not believing the words that came from her mouth, she said aloud, "God, if You are real, make yourself known to me." She sat in complete silence, as she slowly inhaled and exhaled, waiting for a response. After what seemed an eternity, she simply said, "that's what I thought." She started her car and headed back to her motel.

CHAPTER TEN

S arah was 14 years old. Despite the early morning hours, it was hot and muggy outside as her dad began building a patio in the backyard. Sarah never said it to him, but she was in awe of his ability to make something out of nothing. To her, he was the most powerful man in the world – greater than any boy at school. She walked outside, silently observing him as he built. "Hey Sarah, why are you just standing there? Why don't you help?" Sarah couldn't believe what she had heard. She had never worked on a project with her Dad. He was barely around. She could hardly contain her excitement as she went into the house to change her clothes.

As she came outside, she noticed a second toolbelt lying on the ground next to his workbench. Her dad's garage was impeccable, and she was never allowed to touch his tools. He put it around her waist, tightening it snug. "Come on. You want to learn how to build?" "Yes, dad," she said. "You want to learn what a powerful woman you are who can do anything you put your mind to?" "Yes dad," she quietly said again. And the two began to work, the daughter eagerly listening as the father taught.

THAT NIGHT AS SARAH SLEPT SHE HAD ANOTHER NIGHTMARE. IT was Thomas' memorial service, and she approached the church to get inside. As she ascended the steps leading to the front door, she was stopped by the older woman. "Why are you here?" she asked. "You have been told several times that you are not welcome, but you keep coming back anyway. Why?"

Looking at the woman, Sarah's hands shook uncontrollably as she whispered, "but he's my dad. I was invited here."

As she stared at the old woman, the lady became larger and towered over Sarah. "Invited here?" she laughed. "You ungrateful, pathetic excuse for a daughter... You did not want anything to do with him in the last years of his life... you were too consumed with your own hurt to be there for him when he needed you most... and now you want to be there for him after he has died? It is too late. It will always be too late for you."

As the old woman spoke, she became increasingly larger as Sarah crouched to protect herself, paralyzed with fear.

The old lady continued. "Now, out of a sense of guilt, you come across the country to honor your father? That is not what you have called him. He was always Thomas to you. You know that I am right. You cannot deny it," she smiled in triumph.

"I know," Sarah whispered, unable to look the woman in her eyes. "But I believe people can change. I can change."

The woman continued to grow even larger, as Sarah lay on the ground, curled in a fetal position.

"No one can change," she laughed, "especially you. You know deep down inside that I am right. You are weak, and I will always hold power over you. I will always control you."

Sarah could not breathe as her heart began to race violently in her chest.

Right when she thought she was about to die, she noticed out of the corner of her eye Jennifer and Joy open the door to the church, beckoning her to come in. "Sarah," they cried out. "We can help you. Please let us help you."

Sarah stayed in the fetal position, unable to speak as the elderly woman continued to tower over her.

"Sarah," the two women again called out. "We can help you, but we cannot do it without your permission. You must be willing. You must do your part."

"I can't," Sarah sobbed. "I'm not worthy...I am simply not worthy of your help... I can't do it."

As the elderly woman pulled out the knife, raising it high above her head, Sarah was suddenly awakened by the sound of her cell phone.

As she opened her eyes, she slowly adjusted to the reality of her room. She quickly moved her hands to her phone, hoping it was her son but thinking it was most likely Ron. As she turned over her phone, she was surprised to see a call from Jennifer.

"Hello?" she said, yawning.

"Good morning Sarah," Jennifer said excitedly.

"I was not expecting a call from you this morning."

"I was just thinking about you," Jennifer said, "wondering how you were doing?" Before Sarah could respond, Jennifer said, "why don't you look outside your window?"

Groggy, Sarah slowly approached her blinds. As she opened them, she was surprised to see a green van outside with Jennifer leaning against the driver's side door with a cell phone in her hand.

When she saw Sarah, she waved at her. "Are you surprised to see me?"

"Yeah," Sarah responded. "What's going on?"

"Well, don't think you are the only one who can show up uninvited to a person's house," she laughed. "It's Saturday morning. We know it is Thomas' memorial, but feeding the homeless was a big part of his ministry. We wouldn't miss it, especially on this day."

As Sarah continued to wake up, she thought about the conversation she had with Michael the night she had dinner at his house. He mentioned that they would be feeding the homeless Saturday morning and had invited her to come, but she had forgotten about it until now.

"This is your last day here, and we would love for you to come. There will be plenty of time to get ready for the memorial afterward. So, what do you think?"

Sarah thought for a moment and decided that being active that morning would be better than feeling sorry for herself as she was cooped up in her motel room, so she agreed.

"Great," Jennifer said. "Take all the time you need to get ready. We'll be waiting for you outside."

Knowing people were waiting on her, Sarah quickly changed her clothes and brushed her teeth. As she came outside, she noticed Michael behind the wheel and Nathaniel sitting in the back. An additional passenger, an older woman sat quietly next to Nate. As she walked towards the van, Jennifer gave her a long, warm hug.

"Isn't it funny how we just met less than four days ago, Sarah, and we have been in contact every day since your arrival? This must be a God thing."

"Whatever it is," Sarah responded, "it has been nice getting to know you and your family."

"Thank you," Jennifer said, as she opened the door for Sarah.

As she got into the vehicle, she could smell food, and looked back to see a large box of hot dogs wrapped in aluminum foil. Also, there were peanut butter and jelly sandwiches in plastic bags. "Unlike in larger cities such as Redding," Jennifer said, "the homeless population in Burney is pretty low. Depending on the time of the year, we have a lot of transients who briefly come through town, hitching a ride to Mt. Shasta or to Portland, OR. The amount of people we see changes each week, but it's getting colder outside, so the turn out should be less than usual. We should only be out for an hour or so."

Sarah looked over at the older woman sitting in back, wondering who she was. "My apologies. How rude of me? Sarah, this is Joann."

"Nice to meet you," Sarah said, reaching out her hand.

"Joann is one of my favorite people." The older lady blushed and smiled. "Our group first met her over a year ago, isn't that right, Joann?"

"That's right," the woman said, exposing missing teeth as she spoke.

"Joann, would you like to share with Sarah how we met and some of the positive changes that have taken place in your life over the last year?"

"Sure," Joann said. "I would love to. I dunno...where do I start? I haven't always lived on the streets," she began. "I was a stay at home mom most of my marriage. But as I got older, I noticed my husband becoming less attracted to me. I found out he was having an affair with someone from his job. Then one day he came home and told me that he wanted a divorce," she said as if she had told this story many times.

"And he made sure I would get nothing in return. He even

125

turned our kids against me. All I had was my car as I went out searching for any work I could find. I didn't have many job skills. I mostly worked as a waitress and could barely support myself. It got so bad that I lived outta my car."

"I felt hopeless and began to drink. I lost many jobs because of my drinking and just wanted to die. I eventually lost my car and somehow made my way to Burney. I knew it was only a matter of time before my life ended. I hated God and everyone around me, and I just gave up on life, and then one Saturday, I saw Jennifer and Michael and other church members handing out food, clothing, and talking about God." She looked over at Jennifer, who reached over to rub the woman's shoulder.

"Joann is our greatest success story," Jennifer stated. "She started coming to church a few weeks after we first met at the park. She even asked to join a few of our home groups, and she slowly stopped drinking. You will meet someone later today, Sarah - a widowed church member, Mrs. Turner, who has a cottage on the back of her property. She was so impressed with Joann that she invited her to temporarily live in her cottage."

"I love Mrs. Turner so much," Joann said. "We are the best of friends. She even pays me a little money to clean her house, and she helped get me back in touch with my oldest son, Rick. I'm planning on visiting him in a few weeks."

Sarah did not know what to make of the story. She had mostly negative experiences with the homeless she came in contact with at her work, but she tried to keep an open mind.

As the story came to a close, they reached Bailey Park, where a few other church members were praying while walking the perimeter of the park. Michael parked the van, and he and Nathaniel went to the back to get the hot dogs and sandwiches.

As they set up a few folding tables to place the food and

clothing items, they noticed only a few homeless people. In the summertime, the park sometimes had upwards of twenty people to serve, but most had either gone to Redding where there were more resources for the winter or had made their way to other warmer climates.

As the table was nearly set up, a small line of people had formed who were looking forward to a meal. Various volunteers chatted with people whom they had gotten to know over the months, asking them how their week had gone and how they could be of service to them.

As Sarah looked over the scene, she could not help but think of her experiences as a nurse and her interactions with the many homeless and drug-addicted people who had continually returned to the ER and the ICU.

She remembered a particular homeless patient who was admitted to the hospital after nearly dying from an overdose. He was at first despondent, which she understood. She had seen that reaction in many patients in similar situations. But later on, he became overly critical of the staff, refusing to eat the poor-quality food, as he put it, and complaining of the substandard care from the nursing staff. It had always bothered Sarah that people who had so little to begin with could be so critical of others whose job it was to care for them.

Her reverie was broken by Jennifer, who approached her with an older woman Sarah had not met. "Hey Sarah, as you can see, we are just getting started. I'd like to introduce you to Martha. She is a deacon in the church and very passionate about this ministry. I figured you had spent enough time with me over the last few days, so I thought it would be nice for you to meet some new people."

As Jennifer stopped speaking, Martha held out her hand to

greet Sarah. She was a kind-looking woman in her early seventies with short, straight grey hair.

"I need to get back to my family now," Jennifer said. "We'll not be out long today – just a little over an hour or so. I'll get back to you later as we wrap up," she said over her shoulder as she joined Michael and Nathaniel who were serving food.

"Oh," Martha said as she looked at Sarah. "You're Thomas' daughter. I'd heard stories around the church over the last week, and I'm surprised Jennifer didn't mention that to me."

Attempting to change the topic, Sarah talked about what a nice area Burney was.

"Yes, it is," Martha said. "I lived in Southern California most of my life. I moved here after retiring from my profession as a therapist. I loved my work, but I'm glad to be in the next phase of my life. I love the peace and beauty that this environment provides."

"I couldn't agree more," Sarah said. "I really love Mt. Burney and Burney Falls." After walking a few moments, Sarah asked, "So, can you tell me more about this ministry?"

Martha seemed delighted by the question. "As you probably already know, it is something your father began a few years back. He did a good job of getting support from other churches to provide as many resources as possible for our homeless population. For example, one of the area's churches has a large gymnasium behind it. Thomas convinced the church leaders to let us use it for Thanksgiving and Christmas dinners and also as a temporary shelter when it was cold outside. Originally, he used our church, but it was too small and was creating too many problems with the church members, so this solution worked out best for everyone."

"You know," she said as she began to laugh, "your dad could be very persistent when it came to realizing his dream. I saw him get into a tussle with a few leaders in town when they got in the way of his vision. He was not a man to easily back down." Sarah said she had heard similar remarks from others and was inclined to believe it. As they spoke, a homeless lady approached Martha and extended her arms to embrace her.

"Hi, Julia," Martha said as she reached out and hugged the woman. "How's your week been?"

"Very blessed," the lady said. Her recently shaved head was covered in a beanie and her tanned skin was wrinkled from extreme sun-exposure. "I've been able to sleep in the gymnasium this week and have eaten every day. All my needs have been met. I'm grateful," the woman said as she smiled.

"Sarah, I want you to meet my friend, Julia. We've known each other for the last eight months. Is that right?" she said, looking over at her friend.

"It sure is," the woman responded as she reached out and shook Sarah's hand.

"Out of all the people who come out on Saturdays, I've connected with Martha the best," Julia said as she gave Martha another hug.

As the woman walked away, Martha told Sarah part of Julia's story. "When I'd first met her, she was depressed and didn't open up with many people. It took several months of me approaching her and asking her about herself before she finally began to talk freely with me."

"She told me about the morning she knocked on her daughter's door and didn't receive a response. Several hours had passed before she entered her daughter's room and found her lying dead on her bed."

"That's terrible," Sarah said.

"It was devastating. Apparently, the young girl had a congenital heart defect and had passed away in her sleep. Julia never quite recovered and eventually left home and started to take drugs to deal with her loss."

The two continued to walk about the park as Martha continued the story. "Julia told me the incident happened on August 14th, 2005. As that day approached earlier this year, I felt this overwhelming desire to reach out to her. I decided to visit her at this park that afternoon. She was alone, and I could tell she was in a lot of pain."

"She must have been surprised to see you," Sarah said.

"Yes, she was. I'm not sure why, but I felt like I needed to take her out to eat. She couldn't believe the offer, but she gladly accepted. I'd never done anything like that before or since, but you start to connect and love the people you see out here every week. Julia is special to me. Working with these folks has changed me."

Sarah looked away from Martha, shaking her head, letting out a faint laugh.

Looking at Martha, she said, "Well, it seems you are getting a sense of purpose from this ministry. I'm glad you are finding meaning in it."

As the two women continued to walk, Sarah looked out at Michael and his family as they were passing out food and clothing to people. She noticed how engaged they were with those that they served – how happy they seemed to be working together as a family. She looked over at Nathaniel as he worked beside his parents, and she thought about the legacy they were handing down to him, and it made her think about her son, David.

Her thoughts were interrupted by Martha who continued to discuss different facets of Thomas' ministry.

"He did a good job networking with people to create more opportunities to help our homeless population. For example, he partnered with a man from Redding who would come up here every few months with a trailer that had shower-stall units built into it."

"He also connected with the Good News Rescue Mission in Redding and learned about an eighteen-month program they offer to help people with drug abuse and alcoholism." Sarah was surprised to hear the depth to which her father had immersed himself in this ministry.

"Both he and another man from our group would drive people down to the mission if they felt the people were committed to creating a better life for themselves. You will hear a testimony of one of these people today at the memorial service. His name's Corey, and he should be here now," she said looking around. "If I see him, I will introduce the two of you."

"Hey, Martha," Sarah said. "I've been in the nursing field for a while, and I've dealt with a lot of homeless. Aren't you concerned that you are being taken advantage of?"

Martha momentarily nodded her head as she thought of how to respond to Sarah. "Of course," she said. "This work has been a continual learning experience. I can think back to when a couple came to our church asking for money and gas so that they could get to Chico to reunite with their family. They said they were parked behind the bowling alley because they had run out of gas. We helped them but later got a call from another church who told us that the same family came to them later that day with the same plea for help."

"We obviously know there are people who will try to manipulate us. And we always try to make the best decision possible. We don't expect everyone to miraculously be healed from their addiction or even want to stop. Some, if not many, will choose to remain in this lifestyle. Plus, a lot of the people we deal with have mental illnesses, so there's little we can do for them."

"Then why are you out here?" Sarah asked.

"It is because of what God has called us to do as Christians. We come to share our experiences and our hope to help others in need. We make sacrifices by giving of our time and money to help others – even if just a few people will truly benefit from it. Honestly, it's not just about them. We do it for ourselves – I do it for me," she clarified. "It brings me great joy and happiness to give of myself and to bless other individuals."

"Look at Julia," she said pointing over to her friend who was eating a hot dog. "Her life is better because of my intentionality with her. That makes me feel good about myself."

She stopped and stretched out her arms. "That was the most wonderful gift your father gave to me. He taught me how to serve and to love others and in the process how to better love myself."

Sarah contemplated for a moment, considering the homeless plight from a different perspective. Her thoughts were interrupted by an approaching large man she had never met. He was over six-feet with a grey-streaked goatee, and he wore a large cowboy hat. He looked to have been in his late sixties. He was slightly over-weight but looked strong and in good shape for his size.

He approached the two women and introduced himself. "I don't think I've had the pleasure of meeting the two of you. Hello, my name is John. I'm visiting from out of town for Thomas' memorial service." Then looking at Sarah, he said. "I heard you are his daughter. Is that correct?"

"Yes, it is," she replied, wondering what he wanted.

"It is a pleasure to meet you. I was your father's sponsor."

As Sarah looked at the large, imposing man, wearing a

cowboy hat, she felt she knew him from all she had read in her father's journal. Part of her felt slightly ashamed of having read the private and intimate sections of her father's writing regarding John. She knew it was a personal, shared experience between two men that was only meant for them. Keeping these thoughts to herself, she extended her hand. "It's nice meeting you as well.

The gentleman looked at her kindly as he said, "Your dad and I went through quite a bit together. I'm planning on discussing some of those stories later today when I speak at his memorial. Ever since I heard the news of his death, I've been in a state of grief. He's been there through some difficult times for me, and it's the least I can do to come and pay my final respects to him."

"I only wish I had known about his diagnosis. I didn't know he was sick. The only thing I could imagine is he did not want me to worry..." He trailed off, briefly looking around. "But I'm sure he would have been happy that you came."

"I've heard that from a few people this week," Sarah said.

As they continued to speak, Jennifer approached. "Hello, John. I see that you've met Sarah.

"Yes, I have. I searched around for her after I heard she was at the park." Sarah blushed.

"Well, we will be wrapping up in a moment," Jennifer said. "We'll need to get ready for the memorial service, which is just a few hours from now. If you follow me, Sarah, we could use some help picking up after we say our closing prayer."

The remaining time at the park was spent picking up and saying goodbye. Many in attendance wanted to pay their final respects to Thomas, so it was arranged to have a van or two come back 30 minutes before the memorial service to pick them up.

As the green minivan entered the Green Meadows Inn parking lot, Jennifer turned to Sarah. "It was really nice having you with us today. It meant a lot to our family."

"Thank you," said Sarah. "It was a nice experience. I enjoyed my time with Martha. She shared a powerful testimony with me."

"That was just the tip of the iceberg. If you were to come every Saturday, as we do, you would see mighty miracles from God." She rubbed her husband's shoulder before adding, "I'm not sure, but maybe you will hear some more later today at the memorial service."

"Thank you for coming over to our house for dinner and taking the time to get to know us," Michael said. "We are thankful to have gotten to know you."

"You're welcome," Sarah said with a faint smile before getting out of the vehicle.

Jennifer got out of the car and hugged Sarah. "I love you," she said. "I will see you soon, okay?"

"Of course," Sarah said.

As the minivan exited the parking lot, she opened the door to her room and lay on her bed.

What a week it had been for her. She would have never imagined that part of her would be sad to leave Burney. It reminded her of the feelings she had on the last day of camp as friends said goodbye to one another, wondering if they would see each other again. She had only known Jennifer three days, but she felt she knew her better than all of her friends combined at home. She would not admit it to another soul, but part of her was saddened that she may never see her again.

As she reflected on these feelings and the upcoming memorial service, she thought of the time in High School when a fellow student of hers was killed. Adriana Garcia was her name. Sarah did not know her well, but one day after school, the young lady was driving home with friends when her car was hit by a man who had fallen asleep behind the wheel.

The following day when the principal announced over the intercom what had happened, the school was in shock. When you are young, you feel invincible and take life for granted. It was just the day before that she had seen Adriana running on the track with her cross-country team, and now she would never see her again. She was literally here one day and gone the next.

As she lay on her bed engrossed in her thoughts, she began to appreciate life in a way she had not done for many years. Who was it she needed to spend more time with and to tell she loved? Who were the most important people to her? What was her legacy?

As she ran through these questions in her mind, she felt an overwhelming desire to connect with her son. It always hurt when he did not answer, so she usually shied away from reaching out to him, but she wanted to talk to him. She dialed his number and listened as it rang. It went to voicemail, so she left a message: *Hi David. It's your mother. I will be coming back home tomorrow. Today is your grandfather's memorial service. I wish you could be here... I'm sorry if I was a bad mother to you. I hope you can one day forgive me for not being there when you needed me most... I miss you and love you very much.*" As she spoke she began to cry, and she immediately ended the call.

She could not believe the vulnerability she displayed when leaving the voicemail message. She looked at herself in the mirror with her hair frazzled and tears pouring down her cheeks. Looking at herself directly in her eyes she asked, "God if you are real, make yourself known to me." She continued to stare in silence while tears streamed down her face.

"I have made so many mistakes. I have so much regret. I have lost so much. Is there hope for me? Can I change?" she asked pleadingly. "Will I ever be able to reconcile with my son? Will he forgive me?"

She sat in silence as she stared at herself in the mirror.

"Are you there, God?" she shouted, not caring if people from adjacent rooms heard her. After waiting a few minutes in silence, she placed her face up to the mirror so that her nose touched the glass, and defiantly said, "that's what I thought."

CHAPTER ELEVEN

S arah was four years old. It was late at night, and she suddenly awoke to the sound of her father crying. Concerned, she got out of bed and walked next to her parents' room but did not say anything. The door was slightly open, and the light was on. Her dad was in his pajamas with no shirt on, lying on the bed. He was crying. "Where was mama?" Sarah wondered.

"I'm sorry," her father sobbed. "Why did you leave us? I am sorry I couldn't change. Oh God!" he shouted in anguish. "Why couldn't I change? Why did I have to lose her? I loved her so much. Why couldn't I stop? God, please bring her back," he continually sobbed as he held a letter in his hands. Without saying a word, Sarah ran back to her room and put her blanket over her body to protect herself. She held on tightly to her teddy bear, Mr. Grumps while crying in bed.

ON THE GROUNDS OF THE CHURCH WAS A SOLITARY OAK TREE, whose gnarled branches swung ominously above the ancient building, threatening to break off at any moment. Strewn all about were leaves. It looked as if the outside of the church had not been maintained in quite some time.

Sarah could barely make out the church in the distance, which looked to be more than a hundred years old. She imagined a by-gone area in which whole communities dressed in their Sunday best to gather for worship. Yet how the times had changed. This community seemed backward to her – naively holding onto a way of life that no longer seemed relevant, and it made her want to pack up and leave even more.

On her approach to the church, she was surprised to notice cars parked along the road. The small parking lot held room for only a dozen or so cars. She noticed a sign next to the sole empty parking spot, which said: "Reserved for Sarah Martin". She was touched.

As she got out of her car, Jennifer approached her. "How are you doing?" she asked, as she extended her arms in a warm embrace.

"I'm doing fine."

"Glad to hear," Jennifer responded. "I need to go inside to help my husband with some food arrangements. We'll talk soon, okay"

As she walked through the doors, she could smell the musky scent of oak furniture polish from the pews in the sanctuary and saw gaudy old red-carpet that looked like it had been there since the founding of the church. In the entrance was a picture of her dad set on top of a rich, red-colored mahogany wood table, adorned with a basket containing a small bouquet of freshly picked Asiatic lilies, white roses, and mini carnations. She stopped and looked intently at the picture. It had been so long since she had seen him that she did not recognize the smiling old man looking back at her.

As Sarah turned the corner, she was surprised to see her aunt Mindy. With everything that had taken place throughout the week, she had completely forgotten about her.

"Sarah," Mindy called out as she began to cry. "I'm so glad you're here. I wasn't sure if you would come. I tried calling you many times and sent several emails. I was so worried..."

"I'm sorry," Sarah said with a faint smile as she glanced at the kitchen. With everything that had taken place in the last week, she had not considered the possibility of her aunt's arrival to Burney. Feeling a tinge of guilt at having blocked email from her Aunt, Sarah said, "I guess the news took me by surprise and I needed time to process. I'm sorry I didn't get back to you."

"It's okay, honey," Mindy said with tears in her eyes. "I'm just happy you're here. My husband wasn't able to take time off work, so I was the only person from my family who could make it."

She stood silent a moment taking in Sarah. "I know we've had our disagreements...I'm just happy you are here." She reached out and hugged her niece.

"Thank you," Sarah said quickly. "I think the service will be starting soon, and I probably need to get to my seat."

"I would love to talk with you afterward if that would be okay," Mindy stated, slightly disappointed.

"We'll see," Sarah said, glancing back at the kitchen as if searching for someone.

As she moved away from her aunt, she suddenly stopped, briefly lowering her gaze to the floor. Hesitating, she slowly turned around to face Mindy. She walked up and looked her aunt in the eyes. "Thank you for sending me that email. Thank you for letting me know about my father's death. I appreciate it." As her aunt continued to cry, Sarah gave her a quick hug and a kiss on the cheek before heading towards the sanctuary.

The organist finished playing "Jesus Paid it All" as the pastor stood in front of the church to give his opening statements. Then Joy walked up the steps to the podium to speak. She wore a somber, black dress that emphasized her slender physique. Her blond hair with streaks of grey was neatly done up in a French braid. She had dark circles under her eyes, which were brimming with tears.

She was hesitant at first to speak, then said, "I first met Thomas Martin in this very church twelve years ago. He was reserved and shy. At first, I was turned off by his inability to look me in the eyes." Others in the sanctuary looked at each other and laughed. "We barely communicated for weeks. I thought that maybe he was not interested in me, but slowly I noticed changes in him. He started to attend Sunday school and even joined a weekly Bible study. And the more I got to know him, the more I began to like him." She paused – closing her eyes and taking a deep breath.

"I remember our first date. Honestly, I was surprised it even happened. He was very shy. I never thought he would ask me... but we arranged to have dinner at my house." Her eyes were moist from holding back tears but brightened as she continued to relate her story. She paused to laugh. "I had never prepared lobster, but I wanted to impress him with my cooking skills. I had no idea what I was doing. I think I had the TV on, clumsily trying to follow the cook's instructions and flustered because I had waited until the last minute when I noticed one of the lobsters had actually crawled out of the pot and was walking on the stovetop!" The audience laughed. "I thought I had brought the water to a boil, but I must have forgotten to put the lid on the pot. It just stood on the counter looking at me as if to say, 'you had the audacity to try and kill and eat me'?"

"I screamed so loud that Thomas must have heard because he barged into the house to see a lobster dancing around next to the stovetop. Apparently, we were both scared of lobsters, and he yelled too. He quickly grabbed a rolling pin and whacked it on the head." She gave herself a moment to stop laughing. "It was the most memorable date I've ever had. And by the way, I don't think we ever ate another lobster again." She smiled and waited for the laughter to die down. "How I miss those times."

"He shared vulnerable parts of his past that I will not repeat here," she continued, "including his greatest regrets. Yet I never saw that man in him. I saw a new man... a warm, considerate, compassionate, and committed individual who blessed the lives of others in our community." Upon saying this there were a few shouts of "amen" from the congregation.

"One of the greatest gifts Thomas gave me was demonstrating how a man should treat and love a woman. He respected my boundaries and remained in connection with me even though I hurt him by choosing not to marry him."

"For the remainder of our time together, he was my most trusted, safe, and dearest friend, and I miss him dearly. His death has been such a great loss to me. But I feel so fortunate to have had him in my life these last twelve years, and I can speak for others when I say he has blessed many lives immeasurably."

She suddenly stopped speaking and looked around the room until her eyes met Sarah's. With tears coming down her face, she smiled and walked to her seat.

Jennifer and Michael were next to come up on stage. She was the first to speak. "As everyone knows around here, I always called Thomas "Pops". My father died when I was young, and while I had many healthy male role models in my life, I didn't know how much I was missing a father-figure until I met Thomas. We first noticed him at our weekly Bible studies that were hosted in different member's homes."

"As Joy mentioned, he was reserved and hard to get to know at first. He didn't say much about himself, but he was great at asking questions about me and my family. Michael and I felt God telling us to get to know this man at a deeper level, so we invited him to our house on several occasions for dinner, and it was one of the best decisions we ever made."

Jennifer suddenly stopped, bringing her hand up to her mouth and lowering her head. "Here it comes... My husband always tells me what an emotional mess I am," she laughed. "One of my greatest memories of Thomas was his ability to empathize with our son, Nathaniel. As some of you may know, he's dealt with severe low self-esteem and is very shy. Two years ago, he got a role in the school play. He was excited and worked so hard. But on the opening night..." She swallowed, briefly closing her eyes. "He completely forgot his lines. Some of the kids made fun of him and he didn't want to return to school the next day. He felt so embarrassed that evening that we couldn't even get him to come out of his room."

"Michael and I were hurt and didn't know what to do, so we called Pops. You know what? One hour later he showed up at our house with a chocolate cake – can you believe it? - and made us all put on silly birthday hats. When Nate came out of his room, he lit candles on the cake, which said "Happy mistake-day, Nate!" And he stood up and clapped and said, 'Congratulations on not being perfect,' and went over and gave our son a long hug".

"He wouldn't stop hugging Nate as he told him how proud

he was for failing at the play." As Jennifer looked up, she noticed several people wiping tears from their eyes. "I will never forget what he said next. 'Nate, most people will spend their lives running away from failure because they don't like the way it makes them feel. But the only way you will achieve any type of success is by failing. GOOD JOB. I love you, and don't ever forget to embrace and celebrate your mistakes.'

"I am so grateful to have had Pops in our lives," Jennifer said, her voice growing faint as she momentarily closed her eyes. "And I miss him so much." She looked at her husband, signaling his turn to speak.

"I'm a man of few words, but I wanted to share what an impact Pops has had on our marriage," he said as he squeezed his wife's hand. "Only God knows how many times he answered my phone calls at all times of the day and listened as I cried to him – how many times he came over to our house and listened and counseled us through some dark and difficult times in our marriage. I respected and trusted him so much I would do anything he asked."

"He taught me the importance of making time for my son. Today, I take time each week to do a special activity with Nathaniel. It is our father-son bonding time. Thank you for teaching me what it means to be a father," he said looking over at the picture of the smiling, gray-haired man. "And thank you for teaching me what it means to love and to care for my wife." He gently squeezed his wife's hands, looking intently into her eyes before the two went to their seats.

The next person got up and slowly walked to the pulpit. He was a younger man, perhaps in his mid-thirties. He had long, blond hair, which was in a ponytail, and his clothes looked second-hand. Sarah wondered what connection this man could have had with her father as he began to speak.

"My name's Corey," he said. "I met Thomas when he was walkin' the streets with some of the members of this church. It was nice seein' many of you this morning," he said looking over at a few church members. "I've been around this area 'bout three years and have seen people with good intentions come and go who've tried to help people like me, but Thomas was different. Every Saturday, no matter the weather, he'd do his same routine of handin' out food and clothin' and just talk to people. He just wanted to get to know 'em." He stopped for a moment and rubbed the back of his neck, thinking about what to say next.

"I want to share a little 'bout me. I started heroin when I was a teenager. I dropped outta school and had some legal problems, and finally, my parents kicked me outta my home because I stole from 'em and they couldn't trust me no more. But my mom kept reaching out to me. She never gave up," he said, his eyes watering. "She helped get me in a Narcotics Anonymous group, where I started gettin' clean."

"I made a lotta progress and got married to a woman who believed in me and never held my past against me." Tears fell down his cheeks. "Her parents didn't like me, but we got married anyway. Those were some of the happiest times in my life."

"But things changed. We were married 'bout two years when I got news that my mother died, and I felt like my life ended. My wife tried to comfort me, but she couldn't help. I stopped talkin' to my NA friends. I just wanted to numb, and the cravings for drugs came back and overtook me. We divorced, and I felt like my life had lost all meaning, and I just gave up. Somehow, I ended up in Burney where I've lived off and on the last three years. I just wanted to die. Honestly, it's a miracle I'm still alive."

"And then I saw Thomas and his group. I hated every one of 'em at first," he laughed as he looked out over the audience. "I thought they'd abandon me like the others who tried to help. But Thomas kept coming back every Saturday and always made sure to talk to me."

"I'll always remember how he'd tell me that he liked me. I never had a man tell me that before. At first, it made me uncomfortable, so I would cuss him out, and tell him to get the hell away from me. But no matter what I said, he'd always come to me every Saturday and tell me that same thing: 'I like you'. I don't know what it was, but one Saturday he told me that same message and something changed in me, and I started cryin."

"Thomas looked me in the eye and asked if he could hug me. I can't believe I said yes. He hugged me for a long-time and wouldn't let me go. I don't ever remember feeling so loved and safe in my life. I was filthy and stunk, and people usually ignored me, looking down at the ground as I walked by as if I weren't nobody, but he didn't care about any of that. I always felt I was the most important person in the world to him."

"I told him that I wanted my life back and didn't want to take drugs no more. He told me about a program in Redding called the Good News Rescue Mission." He paused as a few people shouted 'hallelujah.'

"He said there was an eighteen-month program for people who were serious about changin' their lives. He'd heard some of the testimonials of people who'd completed the program and believed that it was a great opportunity for me. He said that it wouldn't be easy, but if I was serious about changin' and was willing to do whatever it took, then the program would be my best shot at recovery. He even offered me a ride."

"And that evening he picked me up and took me to

Redding. It was a difficult eighteen months for me, but I kept in contact with him. Even during our breaks when most students would go to their families for a few days, Thomas would come down and pick me up and let me stay with him for Thanksgiving and Christmas. He trusted me," Corey said, crying again. "I felt like part of his family. He was proud of the changes I'd made and always wanted me to make the best of myself."

"Now, I've completed my program." The room erupted in applause. "And I've found work in Redding, but I come to Burney once a month on Saturday to work with the people who've helped me. I never want to forget what was lost because of my addiction. And I always want to give back what was given to me. Thank you."

The final speaker was John. He stood behind the pulpit, scanning the audience as if he were to give a sermon, then spoke. "Most of you do not know me. My name is John, and I was Thomas' sponsor." He paused as he continued to look around the room. "I would not usually mention this fact outside of a twelve-step circle, but I know that he was open with the church and the community regarding his recovery."

"The fruit of his recovery was evidenced yesterday as I walked the streets with members of this congregation who fed and clothed the homeless and addicts. I was deeply impressed at how each member of the team treated every person with whom they spoke with dignity and respect. They treated the homeless and drug-addicts as human beings, as the children of God that they are." He brought up his hand to rub his chin.

"The funniest memory I have of Thomas was when he visited my ranch in Montana. I had recently moved from Oregon after retiring, and I wanted him to see my dream property. One afternoon the two of us walked up a ridge overlooking my property. I would usually ride up on horseback or my ATV, but I thought it would be fun to hike it with my friend. Thomas was in great shape and loved to move on foot. What a mistake that turned out to be."

"We had my dog, Max, with us, who immediately started barking when we reached the crest of the ridge. He saw something moving in the brush ahead. To our astonishment, it was a grizzly bear that was less than a few hundred meters from us. It was my first time seeing one up close, and both Thomas and I were petrified with fear. Now, as you can see, I am a large man, so you would have been surprised to see how fast I moved that afternoon, but Thomas was faster. I kept thinking of the joke of the two men who were running from a bear. You don't have to outrun the bear, the joke states; you just have to outrun your friend. I could not stop thinking I would be the friend who would be eaten." The audience laughed.

"The only thought that kept me calm was that Max would protect us by scaring the bear, but moments later I saw him pass both of us as he reached the safety of the house first. Well, you could say one thing about Max, he wasn't stupid." The audience again laughed. "My wife was met by the two of us in the garage, completely out of breath. She asked what was wrong, but all I could do was whisper in shock, gun – need gun," he said, re-enacting the scene. "If only I knew that would be one of the last times I would spend with Thomas on Earth." His face turned somber as he scanned over the room.

"I remember when I first met Thomas. He may not have had a needle in his arm, and he wasn't living destitute on the streets, but he was in every way as broken and hopeless as some of the people I met earlier today. I think that is why he was so driven in his ministry. He could relate to those he tried to help. He felt that if he could get better, then others had hope as well. He was doing what he felt God had called of him. And I am so proud of the man that he had become."

He brought up his hand to support his chin, as if in deep thought. "I've never mentioned this, but two years ago my wife passed away from a heart attack. I blamed myself for not heeding the warning signs and taking her to the hospital immediately... I still blame myself." As he spoke, tears streamed down his face. "It was the darkest time of my life. I isolated from everyone, including my twelve-step community, who tried reaching out to me with calls and text. I was so angry with God. I just wanted to die."

"Then one evening late at night, I heard a knock on my door. I could not imagine who it would be and was surprised to see Thomas. As soon as he saw me, he reached out and gave me a long hug as I began crying into his shoulder. He told me when he had heard the news, he dropped everything and immediately got into his truck and drove hundreds of miles to comfort me."

"I'll never forget what he said as he held me. 'John, I owe you so much. Thank you for making me the man that I am. I don't know where I would be without you. You are one of my best friends, and I know that if this happened to me, you would be there for me as well. I love you, and I will do every-thing in my power to help you through this difficult time. I'm here for you. I'll always be here for you.'"

"I heard it stated by Jennifer earlier, but Thomas was an excellent listener. He spent the next few days allowing me to express my deepest grief and pain."

"I know the service will be ending soon but allow me to close with this. When my wife was alive, I would get up at 5:00 a.m. every morning and pray for her. Following her death, I stopped this habit. I just couldn't thank God for anything in my life anymore. Nothing made sense. My wife meant everything to me, and she was gone."

"On Thomas' last day at my house, he woke me up at 5:00 a.m. and challenged me to continue to pray. We held hands as I began to thank God for my beautiful wife of thirty-two years, fully expressing everything she had meant to me. I could barely get the words from my mouth as I thanked Him for all the wonderful memories I shared with Karen from the birth of our children to the wonderful date we had just before her death when she told me how proud she was of me."

"Thomas just kept his head down, holding my hands, allowing me to freely express my emotions without judgment or criticism. It was one of the most beautiful experiences of my life. Now every morning, I continue to get up and thank God for Karen and the wonderful blessing she was to me."

"I feel I've learned more from Thomas than he's learned from me. Other than my wife, he was one of my best friends. Thomas, if you can hear me, thank you. I will never forget you." And with that, he walked off the platform.

The service closed as the organist played "What a Friend We Have in Jesus" as people began to get up and walk towards the kitchen.

Sarah experienced so many emotions reading her father's journal and meeting some of his close friends, but what she heard at this memorial service deeply affected her. She felt herself becoming angry and desperately wanted time alone to reflect.

Not wishing to talk to anyone, she quickly walked to her car to leave. As she was getting inside, she saw a note pinned under the windshield wiper on the driver's side. She opened it to see a key taped to the paper. The letter stated: *Sarah, please go to your dad's house. He is waiting for you. You will find him there. Love, Joy.*

"What a nosey woman," Sarah said as she looked at the cryptic message. "What's wrong with her? And what in the hell does she mean that I will find him there," she said, slamming her door? "He's dead!"

Part of her wanted to take the letter and the key and throw it at Joy, telling her to stay out of her business. But as she held the key to her father's house in her hand, she felt an odd sense of gratitude. As much as she didn't want to admit it, she needed this opportunity of seeing his home because it would help to answer important questions she still had nagging in her mind.

She typed the address into her GPS and followed its instructions to a part of town she had not yet visited. She followed an isolated gravel road into a deeply wooded area. She opened a gate that read No Trespassing and briefly considered if she should continue. She then traveled down a small hill to a solitary house on the left.

As she drove onto the gravel driveway, she saw two half-cut wine barrels that served as planters. She got out of her car. It was silent except for the sound of hummingbirds fighting over nectar from the bird feeders hanging from the porch. She grabbed the journal lying on her passenger seat, and with the key in her hand, she approached the house.

As she entered, she noticed it was cold inside. Everything looked tidied up. It was a simply decorated home with a fireplace in the living room and an open-beamed ceiling. She walked towards the hall and turned on the light and then stopped. Throughout the hallway were pictures of her lined along the wall. She saw her two-year-old self at a birthday party with a Winnie-the-Pooh cake that she couldn't wait to devour.

She saw another picture of her in her Ravens softball uniform. She was probably eight years old. She looked further down the hall to see a picture of her when she was twelve that was taken on her mission's trip to Mexico as she was helping to construct a church. She had paint all over her, but she looked happy. As she looked at these pictures, she became overwhelmed with feelings of grief and anger.

"Why did you abandon me, Thomas?" she yelled, balling her hands into a fist. "Where were you when I needed you most? The only thing you loved were the women in your life. Why couldn't you love me?"

She walked to the living room and knocked over the coffee table. She picked up a vase above the mantelpiece on the fireplace and threw it across the room, shattering it against the wall. "You were a dad to Nate. You were a dad to Michael and Jennifer. Hell, you were a dad to a damn drug-addicted, homeless man, but not me? Why weren't you there for me?"

Tears began streaming down her face as she fully yielded to her emotions, releasing pent up feelings she had held deeply guarded since her childhood. She began hyperventilating and her hands trembled as she sat down on the carpet to calm herself. She looked over at the small table next to the front door where she had left the journal.

"No," she thought, not wanting to follow through with her impulse. "It's too painful. I can't do it. Please, God. I don't want to know…"

Reaching out her trembling hand, she opened it to the last section, titled: *Prayers for Sarah.*

CHAPTER TWELVE

S arah was five years old and dressed in her favorite yellow outfit. She was outside the courtroom with her aunt Sandra from her mother's side of the family. She was holding onto her teddy bear, Mr. Grumps when the door opened, and she saw her mother crying. 'What's wrong, mommy?' she asked. Her mother looked at her as she ran her fingers through her daughter's hair. Reaching down to kiss her on the forehead, she said. 'Nothing's wrong, baby. Everything's going to be alright.' 'But why are you crying?' Sarah asked. Her mother reached down, holding her in her arms. 'I'm crying because I am sad. Sometimes mommies and daddies get angry with each other and can't be with each other anymore.'

She looked deep into her daughter's eyes, stroking her hair. 'But when will you and daddy get back together?' Sarah asked. Her mother looked intently at her as another tear streamed down her face. 'Honey, your daddy and I will not get back together. You won't see daddy and me together at our home anymore. I'm going to another home nearby where you will spend time with me each week. It's okay,' she said as Sarah began to cry. 'No,' Sarah pouted. 'That's not fair. I want you and daddy at home forever. I need both of you.'

SHE OPENED THE JOURNAL TO THE FIRST PAGE TITLED: *PRAYERS for Sarah.* It consisted of diary entries written in letter form. She turned to the first entry.

June 1'st, 2010:

I remember the first time I laid eyes on you, Sarah. Your mom and I were sorting out pictures, chronicling her pregnancy with you when she suddenly went into labor. I was so scared as I helped her to the car. It was a miracle we made it as close to the hospital as we did! But you, Sarah, did not want to wait. You were ready to be born, and nothing was going to stop you. I never prayed so hard in my life as I pulled over the car and began helping your mother to give birth. All I could think of was accidentally hurting you as I saw your head come out. I could not stop imagining the umbilical cord strangling you, and I was never so relieved as when I heard your cry. It was the most beautiful sound. I could not stop sobbing as I looked at my baby girl. I will never forget that day, Sarah. It changed me forever.

God, thank you so much for bringing Sarah Lynne Martin into my life on June 14th, 1982. I loved her from the moment she came into this world. I am sorry I did not fully appreciate and value this gift. I ask that you bring people into her life who fully appreciate and love her. May she grow to fully appreciate and love herself.

AMEN.

Flipping to another random section of the journal, she came to the following passage.

September 16th, 2011:

Dear Lord, I miss my baby so much. Will you ever forgive me for what I have done? Will I ever be able to forgive myself? Last week was my grandson's 12th birthday, and the gift I sent him was sent back to me. A note attached to the gift simply stated to stay out of Sarah's life and to never contact her or her son again. She refuses to talk to me. I am not sure what to do. I admit I have screwed up my life, God. I just want an opportunity for her to see the man I have become. This is destroying me.

I want contact with my daughter and grandson, but I must let go. God, please teach me to let them go. Lord, I commit my daughter and grandson's lives into your hands. I pray that you bring people into their lives who can teach them to forgive and to love. PLEASE DO NOT ALLOW THE MISTAKES I HAVE MADE TO TAINT MY DAUGHTER'S FUTURE. I love her so much...

She covered her mouth with her hand, briefly closing her eyes. Slowly breathing in through her nose, she read the following passage:

February 14th, 2012:

Dear Lord,

It has been nearly six months since I last heard from Sarah. I miss her so much. I am daily learning to turn my will over to your care. But it is hard to trust You. I pray that whatever she is doing today that You will keep her safe – that you will love her – that you will bring challenges into her life that will force her to grow so that she fully realizes what a powerful woman she is.

I would give my own life for my daughter, but I know you already have. This is so hard, but I trust that you will provide for her even if I never see it on this side of eternity. I want nothing more than for my baby to have a relationship with You. I love my daughter with all my heart. Into Your hands, I commit her future. AMEN.

With her hand trembling against her lips, and tears streaming down her face, she continued to read.

August 19th, 2013:

I remember when Sarah was 12 and playing Little League Soft-

ball. I had to work late that night. Well, that's the excuse I always gave. I acted out that evening, and by the time I arrived at the game, it was over. Her team had lost, and she felt devastated. I remember her crying on the ride home, something she rarely did. She reached her hand out to me, but I pushed it away. Oh, if only I could go back and change that! We walked through the door, and she said she wanted to talk, but I was so wrapped up in my pain.

I told her that I didn't have time, that I had to go. She sobbed even louder. "Why don't you listen to me, dad? Why don't you ever listen to me?" I just couldn't handle it. I felt such intense shame as I went to my room and shut the door. "I miss mommy," she cried out. "Can you hear me, daddy. I miss mommy. I need her." I wanted so badly to reach out, to hold her and say that everything was going to be okay, but I was scared. I was frightened to touch her. I wanted to comfort her, but I couldn't. I had to protect her.

Sarah banged on the door crying, and I just hunched down on the other side, saying nothing, like a complete COWARD! I justified my actions by saying that was the only way I could love my daughter. Please forgive me, Lord!

Moving deeper into the journal, she came across the following entry.

November 8th, 2016:

Thanksgiving is coming up, and all I can think of is you and David, Sarah. And I think back on my little girl, just a baby, who was pregnant with her first child. You were so young. I am sorry, Sarah, that you felt rejected by your church family. It was the only one you had. I know how much your best friend's parents meant to you. But for them to send you that hateful, judgmental letter, telling you that you could no longer spend time with their daughter... For you to be removed from your youth group... If only I could go back and tell those pastors what I really thought.

You tried so many ways to tell me how you felt, but I would not *listen. Where was I? Why couldn't I have been there to champion you? You needed a father, and I failed you. You needed protection. You needed guidance. You needed my love and support, but I was too self-absorbed to prioritize the most precious gift in my life. You. I wish I could go back in time and hold you in my arms and tell you how much I loved you. That you were going to be okay. That no matter what, I would be there for you. That WE would get through this.*

God has changed me so much, but I still have a hard time forgiving myself for not being there when you needed me the most. I am afraid that I will take that regret and pain to my grave. I hope that someday you can forgive me.

Dear Lord, thank you for my daughter, Sarah. Whatever she may be doing, I ask that you teach her the gift of forgiveness and that there is beauty in the heart of every person despite the terrible things they may have done. They're just hurt people, like all of us, who need our compassion even when we feel they don't deserve it. AMEN.

As she reflected on what she had read, she was surprised by the details of her childhood her dad had remembered. She always thought of him as self-absorbed and an absent father who was rarely at the house and who didn't care about her needs. Yet, he was aware of many of the problems she faced during her pregnancy. How much more did he know?

With these thoughts in mind, she continued to read.

June 14th, 2019

Today is Sarah's birthday, one of the most difficult days of the year for me. I was looking through some boxes of pictures of her when she was a baby and came across one with her next to a Winnie the Pooh cake. I remember her blowing out her candle and then burying her face into the cake. She was covered in frosting as I picked her up in my arms and kissed her on the cheek. She got frosting on me, but I didn't care. It is amazing the memories a single picture can bring. When I look back at that time, it was one of the few moments when I can say I was a good father.

I asked Joy to come over to help me process my emotions. She is such a good friend. As soon as she entered the room, I began to weep and buried my face into her shoulder. 'I've been such a terrible father,' I kept sobbing. 'It's okay,' was all she said. She just let me cry. Then she told me something very powerful. 'Thomas, I feel safe around you. You have told me about your past, but I do not see that man when I look at you. Your daughter would be so proud of the changes you have made. You have developed into the man that she has always needed. You are her father, and you are the bravest man I have ever met.' She gently held my hand as I continued crying. Thank you, God, for bringing her into my life!

We spent the rest of the evening taking pictures of Sarah out of boxes and setting them up throughout the hallway. At the end of the evening, she challenged me to look at those pictures every morning. They would serve, she said, as a reminder of the beautiful human-being Sarah's mother and I brought into this world.

Joy wanted me to remember that I am, and will always be, Sarah's father. And the best way I could serve my daughter would be to pray daily for God to heal her, to reconnect her with that beautiful little girl shown on the picture frames on the wall.

Dear Lord, heal my daughter. Help her to feel loved, to be seen, to feel heard, and to be protected and cared for. Help her to connect with that beautiful, innocent, loving little girl inside of her. AMEN

Sarah set down the journal and paced back and forth throughout the room. She kept her arms folded tightly against her body as she stared at the carpet. She was having difficulty processing the regret her dad felt about not being there for her. How could this be, she thought? Why didn't I see this part of my dad when I was a teenager?

Picking up the journal, she came across the following passage.

March 3rd, 2019:

Dear Lord,

This has been a particularly difficult day for me. I called my sponsor and talked to him for over an hour, but I feel I need to write to process more of my feelings. My ex-wife, Cassandra, filed for divorce when Sarah was five. I was such a terrible man during this process. I was angry with myself, but I turned those feelings towards my ex-wife, blaming her for the dissolution of our marriage.

She was not working, and I was the only one making money. We had a joint bank account, and I took everything out, leaving her with nothing. I'm so sorry. I still cannot believe what I did! I forced her to get help from her parents and a local church just to survive, which made it difficult for her to defend herself during the divorce proceedings. But it didn't stop there.

Before the custody was finalized, I insisted on keeping Sarah as long as possible, doing everything in my power to limit the amount of time her mother spent with her. I didn't care. Nothing mattered to me except having control. I was obsessed with punishing her for the divorce even though it was my fault. But worst of all, I tried to turn Sarah against her mom, telling her that it was her mother who was responsible for breaking up the family.

Cassandra was one of the kindest and sweetest women I had ever met, and I systematically ruined her reputation to the girl whom she loved the most. Not once did she ever say anything bad about me to Sarah. God, can you ever forgive me? I sometimes feel I deserve my fate. It is hard for me to forgive myself.

And later, when Cassandra began dating, I made false accusations, accusing her boyfriend of being abusive towards Sarah. He was a kind man. He was the stable, committed, responsible man that I could not be in my relationship with Cassandra, and I hated him for it. I hated myself. Could I not think of anyone other than me? Was I so full of my own grief, which I had caused, that I would attempt to destroy the life of an innocent and loving mother? God, please forgive me...

There were smear marks on the pages from Thoma's tears as he had written this journal entry. Sarah had never seen this side of the divorce. She loved her mother and was extremely angry that her father would have hurt her that way. At the same time, she also considered the extreme pain that his addiction caused in destroying his marriage to the woman he deeply loved and seeing that same woman with another man. Despite the intense anger she felt towards her father, she had a deeper appreciation for the issues in his life that contributed to his decision making.

She continued to read.

Now comes something I would rather not write. I don't want to think about it let alone put it on paper. Dammit! I've never even discussed it with anyone, not even my sponsor. Only a few people in the family know of my part in it.

It had been two years since my divorce with Cassandra, and I had custody of our daughter on the weekends. It was Friday and Sarah was already at my house when I got a call from a woman who told me her husband would be out of town for the weekend. She said we would have her place just for ourselves. I felt torn, but my cravings took over, and all I could think of was that woman, but I didn't have anyone to watch Sarah. So, like the insensitive jerk that I was, I called Sarah's mother and said things had come up and that she would need to pick up her daughter. Yeah, her daughter!

It was Cassandra's one-year wedding anniversary, and she and her husband were counting on me to watch Sarah, but I told them that wasn't my problem. Why would I have said that? I refused to even look for a babysitter, and I told Cassandra that she would have to pick up our daughter and figure it out. She was so angry that she hung up the phone on me. Honestly, I felt a little guilty, but I let my pride over-rule me. When I look back at it, I was angry that my ex-wife had moved on and was happily married.

It was late that Friday night, and she was driving some windy roads to my house, but she never arrived. I couldn't get a hold of her. God, I wasn't even concerned. All I could think about was her ruining my plans.

I'll never forget when Cassandra's husband called me the following day to tell me what had happened. The police got a call of a vehicle spotted in the marsh off Highway 4. She had gone off the road and drowned. It was late at night and nobody was there to save her! She was trapped in her vehicle all night, and it was all my fault!

Her husband couldn't stop crying as he yelled at me on the phone. All he could say was that he hoped now I could feel good about myself. I had won. Now I could have Sarah all to myself, he said, before hanging up the phone. My daughter eventually found out how her mother died, but for the longest time, all I could tell her when she asked for her mommy was that she was just gone. Why couldn't I tell her the truth? Why couldn't I tell her that I was responsible for her mother's death?

"Damn you!" she yelled as she looked about the living room. "You self-centered son-of-a-bitch," she cried out, clenching her fist. "You are nothing but a coward… a pathetic man, who preyed on innocent people to make yourself feel stronger. How could you have been so selfish and treated my mom that way? SHE DID NOT DESERVE THAT!"

Frightened by the intensity of her emotions, she sat down on the floor, bringing her knees up close to her body as she rested her forehead on her legs. She sat in this fashion for the next few minutes as she continued to cry. She had spent most of her life repressing these emotions, and it was a relief to finally abandon herself to them, giving herself complete freedom to feel.

As she continued to sit down on the carpet, she struggled with how to resolve these feelings of intense anger with the radically different man she had learned about over the last week through his writings and the people whose lives he impacted. As she started to calm down, she thought about the circumstances surrounding the birth of her son.

She was only sixteen when she became a mother. Jake's parents were mortified their son had become a dad at such a young age. They were conservative Christians, and all the talk and gossip was extremely embarrassing for them. They felt so much judgment from their church that they left and joined another fellowship across town. Despite living in a tight-knit community, they did everything they could to keep the circumstances of their grandson a secret from their new church, and from those they came into contact with.

From their viewpoint, it was as if the relationship between their son and Sarah never existed as they kept preparing him for a running scholarship at Oregon State University. They wanted a bright future for their son, and they felt a child and a potential marriage to Sarah would destroy any chance of success and happiness in his life.

Over the next year and a half, Jake was supportive, visiting his son, David but only occasionally. But as was the case with Sarah's girlfriends, when the novelty of a new baby wore off, he became even less involved in her life, and Sarah felt increasingly isolated. Both Jake and Sarah were kids who now had a kid of their own, and they were woefully unprepared for this responsibility.

As their High School graduation date neared, Jake came over to say that he was accepted at Oregon State University and asked Sarah what she thought of him leaving for school. She pretended not to care, but inside she felt hurt. She felt abandoned by Jake, just as she had been by her father. All she told him was he needed to follow through with his dreams and she would remain at home until he returned.

Jake continued with school, but with time, his phone calls and letters diminished until Sarah rarely heard from him. It was during this period that she received a call from a family lawyer stating she was the beneficiary of a trust fund set up by her mother before her death. One day as her father was at work, Sarah wrote him a scathing letter, packed up her belongings, and both she and her son left. She attended a community college to get her Nursing Degree. She never came back home.

Years later she found out that Jake had fallen in love with a woman at college and that following his graduation had married her. They had children together, and he had his own family. But years later as he tried to reach out and to re-establish a relationship with David, Sarah did everything in her power to prevent that reunion.

As her mind drifted back to the present moment, she thought about how her father had manipulated her mother during the divorce proceedings and during the weekend of her anniversary, and she kept asking herself why people hurt others? Why do people do cruel things to those they profess to love? And the answer dawned on her. Hurt people hurt others, especially those they are close to. It is their way of trying to escape and to get control of the seemingly insurmountable pain they feel. It is a hopeless and desperate means of self-protection that inevitably leads to more pain and isolation.

As she continued deep in thought, a wave of grief overwhelmed her as she realized how she had behaved the same way in so many of her relationships. And with this new understanding in place, she could at least put herself in his position and understand in part her father's motivations and behaviors towards her mother.

She sat in this state of mind for a few moments as she glanced down at the journal. There were just a few pages left to read, so she picked up the book at the following entry:

April 8th, 2019:

Heavenly Father,

I am so scared. I just got the report from the doctor stating I have pancreatic cancer. He has given me months to live. I am frightened of dying, but what hurts more is that I may never connect with my daughter and grandson. I want so desperately to share with them the lessons I have learned. I want to see David grow up. I want to see my daughter in a healthy relationship with a man who genuinely loves her.

I have struggled with this issue for a long time, but I finally feel I am ready. Dear Father, I surrender ever seeing my daughter and grandson on this side of eternity. As painful as it is, I have learned that I can love them best by respecting my daughter's wish that I not be a part of their lives. God, this HURTS. I will always be Sarah's father, but I must completely let them go. I trust that you will provide for them in ways I never could. I set aside any claims I feel I have over them. I give up the right to be a part of their lives.

I believe you have completely forgiven me. For her own sake, I pray that my baby, Sarah, learns to forgive me as well. I want her to experience freedom and to truly be the woman You have called her to be. Help her to process the pain in her life so that she may be able to help others who are suffering. Teach her, as you have taught me, the true meaning of life: To give freely what God has so freely given.

I will always be her father. She has complete freedom to choose whom she lets into her life. Until the day I die, I will respect her privacy. I love her with my being.

Goodbye, Sarah. May you continue the process of healing and transformation that the Lord began in me.

Love,

Daddy.

Inexplicably, that was the last entry in the journal. As Sarah sat in the living room holding onto the remaining, tangible memory left of her father, she was again filled with rage. "God, are you there? Can you hear me? I hate my dad, and I don't know how to forgive him. Please help me to forgive him. Please let me know that you care."

After not receiving an immediate response, Sarah got up and walked towards her dad's room. As she entered, she looked at his bed where she imagined he wrote many of those journal entries she had just read. Trying anyway she could make sense of her emotions, she tried to put herself in his position – to better understand his motives towards her and her mother. But no matter how hard she tried, the image of her mother dying alone in her car flooded her mind, and she was overwhelmed with anger.

Just as she was ready to leave the house, she noticed a piece of paper on her father's nightstand. Moving closer to get a better look, she saw it was folded in two, and on the outside was a drawing of a red, misshapen heart. On the outside was written: *For Mommy.* As she held the paper in her hand, she remembered a story her father had shared with her as a girl.

In a rare moment, he opened up about his childhood when telling her of a vacation he had taken with his family at Lake Lemmon in Brown County. It took place in the Bean Blossom Creek Valley on a beautiful peninsula that extended out from the lake where he and his family would go several times during the summer to swim and to picnic. He was about nine years old, and his younger sister was out wading in the water. She bravely moved out further and further from the beach until the bottom sloped downward, and she had trouble swimming back towards the shore. She seemed too scared to yell out for help as she frantically doggy-paddled to stay above the water's surface.

Thomas' younger brother Tim saw his sister in distress and went out to help her. Reaching out to hold her hand, he was not strong enough and was pulled out with her. Their mother, who was on the beach reading a book, quickly got up and ordered Thomas to go out and to save his siblings.

She was afraid of the water, having never learned to swim. She watched helplessly from the shore as her eldest son reached his brother and sister, extending his hand, but the current was too strong, and all three were carried further into the deep water and were pulled underneath by the weight of the others.

Thomas remembered seeing the sun filter through the water above him and the dark, murkiness below. He could have let go of his brother's hand and saved himself, but all he could think of was his brother and sister drowning if he let go. Just as he thought they had all met their fate, a powerful hand shot through the water pulling all three to the surface. It was his father who was off in the distance swimming when he heard the cries of his wife from the shore.

As the kids were brought to safety, they laid on the beach, coughing up water as their dad asked them if they were okay. Thomas noticed his mother still sitting up on her beach towel, unable to say anything with tears in her eyes, transfixed on the children.

At that moment she remembered when her dad told her of an encounter he had with his mother a few years after the incident. He was eleven and had just come back from his church's family camp. There was something throughout the week that was bothering him, and he needed to talk to his mother about it when he got home. He told Sarah how embarrassed he felt as he entered his mother's room one morning. It was during one of those times after his father left the family, and they were not sure where he had gone or when he would come back.

His mother was lying on the bed crying as he walked up to her. "Are you okay, momma?" he asked, feeling angry at his dad for having left once again.

"I'm fine, Thomas," was all she said as she hugged her son. Thomas knew what he needed to say, but he felt uneasy as he looked at his mom. "What is it?" his mom asked.

After a moment, Thomas said, "I just got back from camp, and it got me thinkin' about what happened at the lake a few years ago."

As he stood looking at his mother, he noticed tears in her eyes as she looked down at her mattress. "I know that you love all of us. And I know you are scared of the water. It's okay." And as he stood looking at his mother at her bedside, he said, "If you didn't call out to daddy for help, we would have drowned. You saved us, mommy. Thank you."

His mother reached out, pulling her son close to her as tears ran freely down her face. Reaching into his pocket, he pulled out the letter with the red, misshapen heart on the outside. Inside it read, "You will always be my mommy. I forgive you for everything."

As Sarah continued to kneel at her father's bed with his pillow held tightly against the side of her face, she was overcome with a myriad of emotions. She continued to struggle with conflicting feelings of empathy and anger towards her father. "You hurt me and momma so much. How could you do that? I needed you. My son needed you. I still don't know how to forgive you as you did with your mom years ago."

Continuing in this state of mind, she looked up and scanned the room, noticing a picture of her and her dad on the wall next to his door. It was taken during a camping trip as Sarah proudly displayed a large trout she had caught. Her father looked at her smiling.

She could not stop sobbing as she slid her back down the wall in her father's room, wrapping her arms around her knees as she held tightly onto the note her father had given his mother.

As she rocked back and forth, she started to feel at peace. She stood up, stretching her arms out on his bed, rubbing her fingers against the cream-colored comforter.

"Thank you, daddy...," she cried out unable to complete her sentence. "You were just a little boy...I'm sorry for what happened to you...," but she was again unable to fully articulate her thought as she began to wail, freely expressing her emotions in the safety of her father's room.

She knelt, burying her face into his pillow, taking in the scent of his body. With tears streaming down her face she said, "Dad.... daddy, I forgive you! Just as you've forgiven your own mom, I forgive you. I love you... I wish I could've seen the pain you were in. I was too wrapped up in my own problems to see your hurt. God, there was so much I didn't know about you. If only I'd known. If only I could've been there for you. Forgive me for not letting you see my son," she said. "I didn't know how much you loved and wanted us in your life. I didn't know the emotional toll it took on you."

"Forgive me for destroying your car and leaving the house and never coming back. If only I could go back and do things differently. Please forgive me, daddy. I love you so much. I forgive you! I forgive you," she sobbed, as she continued to bury her head in his pillow. "Thank you for forgiving me."

Sarah was startled when she heard the doorbell ring. Wiping her tears, she walked down the hall and peeked around the corner but couldn't see who was on the other side of the door. The doorbell rang again. It was dark outside, and she reluctantly went to the door, asking who was on the other side. "It's me, Sarah," Joy said. "May I come inside?"

She opened the door, and the two women stared at each other in silence as the light of the full moon filled the sky.

"Sarah, what's wrong? Are you okay?"

Sarah reached out her hands and hugged Joy, burying her face in her friend's shoulder. They held each other in the silence of the night as the wind rustled the branches of the trees.

"Sarah, it's okay. You're going to be okay. Hey, you want to go inside. I'm sure you're thirsty," she said as she rubbed Sarah's back. "Common, let's go inside."

Joy walked to the kitchen to get the two a glass of water while Sarah sat down at the dining room table with her hands supporting her forehead.

"I'm so glad you came here, Sarah. I imagine this has been an emotional day for you. I hope I wasn't too intrusive coming here tonight."

Sarah continued sitting at the table in silence, moving her face up and down in the palm of her hands.

"Look, honey. I can go. I just wanted to make sure..."

"No, stay," Sarah said, her voice raspy. "I, um...wanted to thank you for all you've done for me this week. I...was so rude to you the other day."

"Don't worry about that, Sarah. It's understandable."

Sarah leaned up in her chair, looking at the empty crystal vase in the middle of the table.

"Don't take this wrong...I really appreciate it," Sarah said, "but why would you have given me my dad's journal? I don't know if I ever could've done that for a complete stranger."

Joy walked to the dining room with glasses in hand as she turned the question over in her mind. "I've known your dad a long time. I never opened that book, but with how honest he was with me, I probably knew most of what was inside it. When I heard you were in town, I knew you needed to have it. Call it God or intuition...I just knew that's what your dad would have wanted."

Joy took a sip of water, watching Sarah who was massaging the back of her neck.

"I guess I didn't want you leaving thinking your dad was only that man from your childhood. I wanted you to know who he became." She remained quiet, letting the richness of the silence communicate what no words were sufficient to do.

"I wasn't expecting any of this," Sarah said, turning to face Joy. "I don't know what to say. I feel so confused. It's too much. I didn't realize how much he..." Sarah lowered her gaze, bringing her hands up to her face.

"Oh, honey, don't worry. It's okay" Joy said, reaching out to touch Sarah's shoulder. "You don't have to have everything figured out right now. Just be in the moment."

Joy moved her chair next to Sarah, putting her arms around the woman's shoulders.

"Hey, Sarah. I need to tell you something. Maybe I should've told you earlier, but with everything that's happened this week... And I know you'll be leaving tomorrow." She cleared her throat. "Sarah, this used to be your grandmother's house."

Sarah remained silent, letting the words linger in the air. She shifted her body as she looked at Joy. She tried to speak, but nothing came out at first.

"I don't understand," was all she could say for a few moments. "I...um...was there for her funeral in Indiana with my dad. She didn't live here."

"Sarah," Joy said, rubbing her companion's shoulders. "It was during the funeral that he found out his mother had asked to be buried in Brown County where she'd grown up. Your family was so secretive that there was little talk about where your grandmother had moved. To this day, some of the family still don't know that she lived in Burney."

"This is all so confusing. It doesn't make any sense. My family doesn't make any sense."

"I know how you feel," Joy said. "This is all so new to you. Let me tell you what I know. Your father told me that his mom left the family when he was in his late teens. After your uncle Tim had died, something changed in her, and she ran away. The family hadn't heard from her in several years. Your dad felt so abandoned and resentful that he wanted nothing to do with her. She even tried to reach out on a few occasions in his early twenties, but he refused any form of contact with her. It was something he regretted most of his life."

"Even many years later when your grandmother had passed, he told me the funeral was difficult for him to attend, especially with the family dynamics. There were many secrets, and most of his siblings didn't want to talk to each other. But it was at the funeral that he realized he still had a lot of resentment towards her. He thought that he'd let much of it go, but he was wrong."

Sarah stared at the cup of water in front of her, running her index finger along its brim. "How did my dad come to buy this home?" she asked.

"He decided to come to Burney to see where she spent the remaining years of her life. While he was visiting, he found her old home up for sale. She'd passed long ago, and while talking to the current homeowners, he mentioned that his mother was a previous owner."

"They told him they'd come across some personal belongings in a box in the attic they thought would be of interest to him. To your dad's surprise, they handed him a box with his name on it, and inside was your grandmother's journal. It mentioned her regrets at leaving the family and other mistakes she'd made throughout her life."

Sarah could not help but think of everything she had learned from her dad in a few short days reading his diary. She wondered if her dad had a similar experience with his mother.

"It wasn't long after that discovery that your father felt he needed to buy this home. It was his way of staying in connection with her and saying that he had forgiven her."

Joy got up to go to the kitchen to get another glass of water, leaving Sarah alone in her thoughts.

"He told me that reading her diary is what inspired him to document his own recovery," Joy said from the kitchen. "He was hoping that it would somehow help others in their journey. It was part of his legacy, as he liked to say. And that's why I knew I needed to give it to you when you came into town."

"And this house is mine?" Sarah said, standing up, taking in the view of the living room.

"Yes, Sarah. When your father found out he had only months to live, he met with a lawyer from our church – Tom Jenkins – and they drafted a will that gave the deed of the house to you when your father died."

"I can't believe this," Sarah said. She looked at the pictures of herself lined in the hallway. "And I told him I wanted nothing to do with him," she said, taking a deep breath. "He didn't even know what I would do with this house."

"I know," Jennifer said. "He told me you'd returned some gifts he'd sent you and your son, and he didn't know how you'd receive this inheritance. But he wanted to at least leave something for his grandson."

Sarah felt a wave of shame rush through her body like a cold draft on a rainy day. How long would she have to deal with these emotions, she thought. Months? Years? She looked at her younger self in her Raven's baseball outfit and began to cry.

"I didn't know...If only I had known what he'd gone through. If only I'd known how much he'd changed and wanted to connect with me."

"Oh, honey. Don't do that. You can't win that game. Don't worry about the 'what-ifs. What's done is done. The important thing is that you came here. You faced some of your fears by opening up the journal and by choosing to stay throughout the memorial service. Focus on what you've done. You can't change your past, just your present."

"But I've made so many mistakes, Joy. You may think you know me, but I don't know how I'm going to change."

"Look, Sarah, there's always hope, no matter what you've done. You may not believe this right now, but you're a powerful woman. You get to choose what you want out of this life. If there's anything I've learned from your dad, it's that no matter what we have done, there's always hope for a better future if we believe in ourselves and reach out for help. You can do it."

"Choose? What do you mean?"

"Sarah, what happened in your dad's life was a miracle. He painted a good picture of what he was like before, but I never saw that man. The man I knew was kind, brave, giving, and Godly. He was beautifully flawed, and he owned up to his mistakes."

"Sarah, the most important lesson I learned from your dad is that we can't change the facts of our past, but we can change the meaning we give them. He couldn't change that he was an addict or that he'd hurt people he loved. But he chose to reach out for help, doing everything his sponsor asked of him, and in the process he found God. He chose to believe that this powerful and loving God could change him if he learned to live in obedience. It was a decision he made every day for the rest of his life. He wasn't perfect, but you heard at the memorial service how those daily decisions positively impacted others."

Sarah leaned against the counter in the kitchen with her hands in her pockets as she looked at the ground.

"Hey, Sarah. You know your dad was proud of you, don't you? Just never forget that he wouldn't want you to be stuck in regret and self-loathing. He would want you to forgive yourself and to find meaning and purpose in your life. Sarah, you're going to be okay. I have a lot of hope for you."

"Hope? How?"

"Don't worry about it just now. You'll figure it out. Just promise to keep in touch with me when you get home, okay?"

The two women reached out and embraced, allowing the healing power of touch to wash away years of regret and to provide endless possibilities for a more beautiful horizon.

EPILOGUE

"God, grant us the serenity to accept the things we cannot change, the courage to change the things that we can, and the wisdom to know the difference," the group recited in unison, following the twelve-step meeting. Sarah looked to her right as her sponsor gently squeezed her hand while smiling affectionately at her.

Following her return to Chicago, Sarah decided to join an Alcoholics Anonymous group through the encouragement of Joy, whom she talked to twice a week. It was extremely uncomfortable when she first walked into St. John's Episcopal Church, so she decided to arrive a few minutes late to avoid meeting any of the members.

As she entered the building, she was not expecting so many to be in attendance. Everything inside of her was screaming to leave – to go back to the comfort and safety of her home. As she was contemplating these thoughts, however, she heard the guest speaker who had already begun sharing her story with the group. Sarah sat in the back pew and listened.

"I was first molested by my uncle when I was ten years old," the speaker said. "This would continue until I was sixteen when I finally had the courage to tell him I wanted him to stop, and that I would tell my parents if he didn't leave me alone. I never told them, though. I kept so many secrets from them."

"I spent most of my teenage years finding love through being sexual with boys. But when that wasn't enough, I began drinking. When I was drunk, I felt free from all the loneliness, pain, and rejection. Everyone loved me, or so I thought."

As the woman continued to speak, Sarah was transfixed by her words and eager to hear more. Even though their stories were not the same, she felt a powerful connection with this person.

"What followed," the woman continued, "were two abortions and a DUI. Well, that was the only time I got caught, anyway." The audience laughed in recognition. "I was twenty-one, and my life wasn't going anywhere. Men only wanted one thing from me. I didn't have a place to live, and I couldn't stop drinking no matter how hard I tried. I felt I was on the course to an early death, and I didn't care."

As Sarah scanned the room, she could feel the love and respect for this speaker. It seemed as if everyone there, in one sense or another, could relate to the woman as she shared intimate and vulnerable parts of her life. What was most refreshing to Sarah was the lack of judgment or criticism she perceived as she looked at those in attendance.

"Then one day, I was alone in my room with a gun to my head," the woman said. "I told God that if he truly existed and loved me, to show me a sign. And just as I was about to pull the trigger, my cell phone rang." There was a gasp in the room from a lady in the front pew.

"I couldn't believe it. Who would be calling me, I wondered?

I reached down to pick up my phone but didn't recognize the number. Curious, I answered the call, and it was a pastor from a nearby church I had visited weeks earlier. He told me God told him to pray for me and to give me a call. Even though we had only met once, in obedience, he contacted me."

"Since I was ten years old, I'd never cried. But when that man reached out in love to me, it was as if all the years of repressed emotions let loose, and I couldn't stop sobbing to him on the phone. That was the first time a man genuinely cared for me beyond what I could offer him sexually."

She stopped a moment to let her message sink in. The room was silent. "I decided that day my life had a purpose," she said, reaching up to wipe a tear from her eye. "There was a God, and there were kind, loving, and safe men who genuinely cared for me. And that's when I decided to join A.A. I immediately got a sponsor and began working the steps, and today marks the twentieth anniversary of my sobriety."

As the audience clapped, Sarah was moved to tears. She decided to talk to that woman following the meeting, and it was the start of a beautiful sponsor-sponsee relationship.

Presently, Sarah looked over at her sponsor, Nicole, and returned the woman's gentle squeeze of the hand and affectionate smile. As people were saying their goodbyes and leaving the meeting, Sarah looked at the purple and silver-plated sobriety chip, signifying her six months of abstinence from drinking and sexually acting out, and she was overcome with tears. Sarah had learned in her short time in recovery to openly express her emotions as tears freely fell down her face.

It had been, to say the least, a challenging and trying six-months. When Nicole told Sarah she would have to forgo all romantic relationships with men for at least one year and to instead focus on friendships with women, Sarah became very upset. As she reflected on her dad's journal entries, however, and his struggles throughout his twelve-step journey, she finally accepted this was the right path for her.

Ron took it hard at first, begging her to reconsider her decision, saying he would get a job and start contributing. But Sarah had already made up her mind, and with the support of her sponsor, Ron moved out. She had not spoken with him since.

What was most challenging was letting go of friendships with people she had met at bars. She didn't realize how co-dependent these relationships were. At first, she felt lonely and wanted to go back to her old patterns to bring her comfort. With Nicole's help, she found healthier ways to get her needs met. She learned the power of being of service to others, mostly through taking calls from women in the program who were struggling. Not only did she find happiness in helping people, but her desire to act out diminished.

The longer she remained sober, the more fulfilled she felt. She could not remember feeling so happy and at peace. She had solid friendships, was of service to others, and she was learning to be honest with herself and to trust in her Higher Power.

SARAH REGULARLY CALLED JOY, WHO KEPT HER UP TO DATE WITH what was taking place in Burney. Michael and Jennifer continued to lead the homeless ministry, which was going strong. They had reached out to Sarah to invite her to visit in the Fall before it began to snow with the promise of taking her up Mt. Burney. Sarah was thrilled with the idea and had booked a round-trip ticket.

She had received documentation of the will from her father's lawyer, giving her the deed to the property. She thought about moving to Burney but decided she would remain in Chicago where she had a career and a strong support system.

After much consideration, she decided to coordinate with the church in Burney to rent to a family who experienced long-term sobriety and achieved financial stability but needed housing. She believed it was what her father would have wanted. This was a short-term proposition. She would either move into the house at a later date or sell it and put the money in a trust fund for her son.

Despite her sobriety and new-found purpose in life, Sarah dearly missed her son, David. When she had initially come home from Burney, she reached out to him almost daily, striving for a connection, but he never returned her messages. It was only through sharing her struggles with the group and her sponsor that she was able to process her emotions regarding her son.

But no matter how hard she tried to let go of David, she still missed him. A few nights earlier, she had a dream where she was at a Christmas gathering at her house along with David's family. Her granddaughter, Kayla, sat in her lap as Sarah helped the girl open her presents. Just having Kayla close to her as the girl excitedly opened her gifts brought Sarah to tears. She loved her granddaughter with all her heart and deeply wanted a relationship with her.

As Sarah woke up late that night and looked around her dark and empty room, she felt sad. Despite her attempts at letting go, she still desperately missed her family and wanted to reconnect with them.

It was 2:30 a.m., and Sarah could not go back to sleep. Instead of feeling sorry for herself, she opened her journal and began to write. She currently was on step nine. She had previously created a list of people with whom to make amends, and now she felt ready to write a letter to her son. She turned on the lamp next to her bed and opened the drawer to get her journal. Embossed on the leather cover was written: For Sarah - a forgiving, bold, and vulnerable woman who humbly seeks God's guidance.

As she leaned against her headboard with her pillows cushioning her back, she wrote: **Step Nine - Amends**

July 23rd, 2020

David,

I am in a 12-step program for alcoholism and other issues in my life. I would imagine you are surprised to hear this information. I didn't even know I had these problems until I visited Burney, CA last December for your grandfather's memorial service. But I will get back to that shortly.

You would be proud that I recently got a six-month sobriety chip. I never thought it possible. I still can't believe all the wonderful, life-changing experiences I have had on this journey in such a short time, and I am grateful for what is to come.

I know you never met him, but I learned a lot about your grandfather during my trip out west. Ever since I was a teenager, I hated him, and I resolved never to see him again and for you never to know him. I thought I was protecting you from a person who deeply hurt me when I was a girl.

But when I got to Burney, a dear friend of mine gave me your grandfather's recovery journal, which I have now read entirely. Who

I once thought a selfish, cowardly, neglectful, and weak man, turned out to be somebody completely different. Was I ever wrong!

The truth is that he was one of the bravest, most courageous, fearless, loving, and sacrificial men I have ever known. The tragedy is I didn't get to know who he was until he passed away. David, receiving that journal was one of the greatest gifts in my life. It helped me to reconcile with and to truly love my father. It helped me to forgive and to ultimately love my dad in ways I never thought possible. It helped me to understand the pain I had so meticulously hidden and was oblivious to for most of my life, and to ultimately seek the help I so desperately needed. I can now say I am proud that God gave me Thomas Martin as my father.

You would have liked him. I wish you had gotten to know your grandfather when you were a boy. He was an excellent problem solver. He was skilled with his hands. He could build anything, and I see those same gifts in you. There is so much of him in you!

He started a homeless ministry and helped countless people come to Christ. He helped to restore marriages. He gave comfort to people when they were hurting. Most importantly, he understood he could not change his past, but he could leave a legacy that would bless others far beyond his death.

One of the greatest lessons I learned about your grandfather was that he came to terms with the pain he caused to so many people in his life, and he asked God to forgive him. He was willing to go to any lengths to follow God's calling. He wanted to live in His will. So, despite all the pain he experienced throughout his recovery journey, he kept moving forward even at the end of his life when he realized he would be dying and would never speak to us again. David, he wanted his legacy to bless both you and me. That was his prayer to his dying day.

That is in part why I am writing to you. I am carrying on your grandfather's legacy, and I am doing that first by apologizing to you for what a neglectful mother I have been.

I was so wrapped up in my problems that I couldn't see how much you needed me, and for that I am deeply sorry. All you knew growing up was a series of men that I met at bars who came and went from our home. OUR HOME, HONEY. Sometimes they would stay a few days or a few months. Some were nice, but most didn't care about you or me, and some were cruel.

David, it hurts me to write this. I have done everything to forget about it - to pretend it never existed. It's still too painful for me, but I need to write it. Honey, I remember the time I walked in on my boyfriend molesting you. I am sorry. I lied to myself for so many years afterward, pretending he was just showing you affection - that he was loving you. I didn't want to believe I was responsible for bringing a man into my home who could do such a heinous thing to my son. I am extremely angry with myself. Why would I have allowed that to happen? Why wasn't I there to protect you? I was your mom, and you needed me. You tried to reach out, but I wouldn't listen to you. I allowed that man to stay in our home another two months while I remained in denial. I was only thinking of myself.

David, I would give anything to go back and to change things. I was a very sick woman. I was not emotionally stable enough to give you the support you needed. I failed you as a mother, and you have every right to never talk to me again.

God has forgiven me. I have forgiven myself. I hope that someday you can forgive me as well. That does not mean you have to be part of my life. As I learned from my dad, I love you enough to give you your space and to allow you to decide what you feel is best for you and your family. I just don't want you to be resentful towards me for the rest of your life. I want you to live in freedom!

I pray for you, Andrea, and Kayla every day. My heart's desire is that you come to know God as I have and that you allow Him to bless your life. I want you to find freedom and blessings, and I don't want anything holding you back from reaching your potential.

God bless you, son. I want you to know how proud I am of you. You are one of the best things that has ever happened in my life, and no matter what, I will always be your mother, and I will always love you.

Love,

Mom

As Sarah placed the stamp on the envelope and put it in the mail, she felt an overwhelming peace permeate her soul, and she began to cry. "Thank you, God," she said as she walked back into her house. "No matter what happens, I give the outcome to you."

SARAH CONTINUED TO FOCUS MORE INTENSELY ON HER recovery. As she moved forward in her step-work and shared her progress in group meetings, she increasingly had more women come to ask for her phone number. She would go out to coffee and listen to these ladies and do her best to provide comfort by sharing her testimony and working through the steps with them.

Some would listen politely, and she would never hear from them again. Others would show signs of growth, only to relapse and leave the group, while others would diligently work their program and find much-needed relief from their addictions. There were not any guarantees, however. There were those who despite their best efforts at following the program principles and turning their lives over to God, would continue to fail. She grieved over this group of women more than any other because they had a genuine desire for change but were continually met with failure. There was no way of predicting who would maintain sobriety and who would not.

Despite the success and failings of those around her, Sarah was resolved to follow her program and to do everything in her power to stay in daily contact with her Higher Power. She was fully committed to her sobriety.

SARAH STILL WORKED IN THE ICU DEPARTMENT AT METHODIST Hospital of Chicago. One day during her lunch break, she spotted her co-worker, Grace, who had just sat down to eat.

"Hey Sarah," Grace said, as she saw her friend enter the cafeteria. "I saved a place just for you. Come sit with me."

Following Sarah's return from Burney, Grace noticed a change take place in her co-worker. She observed a new-found vulnerability in Sarah and an unshakeable desire to improve her life. She made it a point to sit with Sarah at lunch when-ever possible, hoping to get to know her friend at a deeper level.

"How's it going?" Sarah said as she sat at the table.

"Not bad. I'm so happy that young man got off the venti-lator yesterday. It was wonderful to see him communicating with his family" She was referring to a young Hispanic man, Eric Suarez, who had gotten in a car accident. He was on his cell phone texting when he collided with another car. For a while, the medical staff thought he would die, but his family came to the ICU every day and prayed for him. Miraculously, he squeezed his mother's hand a few days earlier and was now breathing on his own.

"I know, Grace. It was beautiful, and I couldn't stop crying.

I wish things turned out like that more often." The two sat eating in silence for a few moments.

"Sarah, last time we spoke, you told me you were working on your 9th step - amends. How's that coming along?"

"Awkward, to say the least, and extremely uncomfortable at times. A few days ago, I met with an ex-boyfriend at a restaurant and read my amends letter to him at the table. I couldn't even make eye contact as I read. It was very painful."

"I'm glad you did it. How did he take it?"

"Not too well. I think he was hoping that somehow we would get back together, but when I finished the letter, he realized the relationship was over. Sometimes I don't like this recovery journey. I've spent so many years unable to tell men 'no' because I didn't value myself. I had no idea what boundaries even meant until I joined this program."

"I'm proud of you, Sarah. The changes you've made over the last nine months have been remarkable. You are a completely different woman. You inspire me."

"Thanks," Sarah responded, blushing. "I don't always feel inspirational. I struggle with things like any other person. But something changed in me after that week in Burney. After I realized how wrong I'd been about my father, and how much I didn't know about myself, I knew I needed to change. I never want to return to that woman who first arrived in Burney. Life's too short."

"I had a similar experience, Sarah, when I saw my dad on his death bed," Grace said. "Most of my life, I only knew him to be explosive, abusive, and neglectful, and I was afraid of him. But when I saw that frail man dying on the hospital bed with IV's hooked up into him, something changed. I knew I needed to forgive him, and it was the best decision I ever made. It sounds like you have done that with your father as well."

"Yes, I have," Sarah said with tears in her eyes. "But I miss my son, Grace. I want him to forgive me and to come back into my life. I'm learning to use this pain as a teacher for how to move forward in relationships, but some days are harder than others."

"I know, Sarah. I can't imagine how painful this is for you. Letting go sometimes is the hardest thing to do, especially when we have no idea what the outcome will be."

As the lunch break came to a close, the two held hands as Grace gave a quick prayer for her friend. "Lord, thank you for Sarah and all the magnificent changes that have taken place in her life. I'm grateful she is comfortable sharing such intimate details of her life with me. I love her. Bless her through this uncertain time with her son and teach her to use this pain to become more sensitive to the boundaries and needs of others. AMEN."

"Thank you, Grace, for listening to me. Thank you for being my friend."

"Of course. Your friendship means a lot to me too."

Later that evening as Sarah returned from her twelve-step meeting, she was exhausted as she entered her home. She walked straight to the shower to clean up before going to bed. As was her custom, she went to her nightstand drawer to pull out her Bible and read a chapter. Then she prayed for her friends and family before going to sleep.

After turning out her lights, however, she felt restless and got up, wandering about the room. She was overcome with grief and began crying. "Oh God, why can't I be with my son? I know this seems selfish, but I miss him. Am I somehow being punished because of the way I treated my father? Is this payback?"

Feeling trapped by the pain in her mind, she walked about

the room, thinking of anything to lessen her emotions. "I keep turning this situation over and over again to You, God. When will this cycle end? When will it be enough? I know I've made mistakes, but I'm in recovery. I'm helping other women in their journeys. I forgave my dad, but I don't want to lose my son over my past sins."

Desperate for relief, she turned on the light and looked at herself in the mirror. With her nose touching the glass, she said resolutely, "I love you, Sarah. You are a fearfully and wonderfully made woman, and God is proud of you. You have done what few have done before you. You have sought help, and you are sober. You are blessed with friendships, a great career, sobriety, and a relationship with God. You have more than enough. You have everything you need."

As she spoke, she was overcome with a feeling of peace. "Lord, no matter what the outcome is with my son, I love and worship You. My decision to serve You will never be based on my emotional state or the results in my life. I trust You. You are my God." As she continued to look at herself, she began to weep.

Overcome with exhaustion, she went to her bed and laid down. She was just closing her eyes when she heard her phone vibrate and saw the light flash from its screen. Wondering who would be calling this late at night, she looked at the phone and was astonished to see a call from her son...

ACKNOWLEDGMENTS

This story has been in my heart for the last three years, but it was only over the last three months I have had the courage to put it into writing. Having dealt with addiction and the loss of many meaningful relationships due to my actions, I wanted to give the perspective of a man who despite his mistakes, learned to forgive himself and to transform his life to bless countless others. It is a story of redemption I hope to aspire to.

I want to thank everyone who has helped make this dream a reality. Thank you Dad for meticulously proof-reading each page and giving me ideas on how to expand the story. And thank you, Mom, for being there for me even in the most difficult of times. I deeply appreciate your unwavering love and support. I also want to thank Michael Kunz who possesses all the goodness exhibited in Thomas but who did not have to experience that character's tragedies to develop into that man. Thank you for patiently teaching me to be a man. You are a role model for many people, and your legacy will be far-reaching through the lives of countless people. God bless you.

I also wanted to thank Lisa Vest and Jennifer Mandigo for editing this book. Your eye for detail helped to clearly get what was in my heart onto paper. And thank you Lisa for your many suggestions that helped open new avenues I had not imagined (namely, the Epilogue). The book would not have been what it is without your help. Thank you very much!

Whether this book is read by a few or many, I hope that it will inspire people to reach for their dreams, no matter how unattainable it may seem. Never let fear or doubt get in the way of expressing your gifts to others. May you boldly design and execute your legacy daily so that others may have a better and more fulfilling quality of life. In so doing, you will bless your life as well.

Made in the USA
Columbia, SC
06 April 2021

35230005R00114